'You've bee
day,' Amy sa

'You've been ve...
replied.

Amy smiled. A smooth talker. He was probably very good at kissing too.

'I've been thinking about that myself,' he said.

'About what?' Amy murmured.

'About this.' He moved closer, bent his head and touched his lips to hers. Amy Brooks, absent without leave from her engagement party, was kissing a total stranger in the summer house. And she had been right. He was very, very good.

He drew back from her lips slowly. 'There must be something in the air. I hear that Nigel is announcing his engagement to some poor woman tonight.'

The observation had all the effect of a cold shower. 'He is,' Amy confirmed curtly. 'And I'm the poor woman.'

Alison Roberts was born in New Zealand, and, says, 'I lived in London and Washington DC as a child and began my working career as a primary school teacher. A lifelong interest in medicine was fostered by my doctor and nurse parents, flatting with doctors and physiotherapists on leaving home, and marriage to a house surgeon who is now a consultant cardiologist. I have also worked as a cardiology technician and research assistant. My husband's medical career took us to Glasgow for two years, which was an ideal place and time to start my writing career. I now live in Christchurch, New Zealand, with my husband, daughter and various pets.'

Recent titles by the same author:

TWICE AS GOOD
A PERFECT RESULT
AN IRRESISTIBLE INVITATION

NURSE IN NEED

BY
ALISON ROBERTS

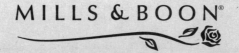

All the characters in this book have no existence outside the imagination of the author, and have no relation whatsoever to anyone bearing the same name or names. They are not even distantly inspired by any individual known or unknown to the author, and all the incidents are pure invention.

First published in Great Britain 2001
Harlequin Mills & Boon Limited,
Eton House, 18-24 Paradise Road, Richmond, Surrey TW9 1SR

© Alison Roberts 2001

ISBN 0 263 82664 3

Set in Times Roman 10½ on 12 pt.
03-0501-46394

Printed and bound in Spain
by Litografía Rosés, S.A., Barcelona

CHAPTER ONE

RED and blue lights flashed their signal of an emergency.

The ambulance siren had been turned off on the final approach to the hospital but the beacons were still going as the vehicle turned swiftly and backed up to the doors of Christchurch's Queen Mary Hospital's Emergency Department. The day-shift resuscitation team stood waiting. The medical staff hadn't needed the warning lights of the ambulance to notify them that a critically ill patient was incoming. That information had been transmitted *en route* ten minutes ago, and the team had rapidly assembled and prepared one of the highly equipped resuscitation areas in the emergency department.

Senior Nurse Amy Brooks cast a swift glance into Resus 1 as the stretcher was being unloaded. IV fluid bags were hanging, their giving sets already primed. Trolleys stood ready. The staff knew their patient was in severe respiratory distress. Equipment for intubation and ventilation was available. A chest-drain tray was prepared and draped.

As the circulation nurse on the resus team, it was Amy's responsibility to have all the equipment prepared and to assist the doctors in using it. She needed to have the IV fluids ready and to assist with or insert IV lines herself, if necessary. She needed to help other nurses to remove the patient's clothing and to record baseline observations of temperature, pulse, respiration, blood pressure and cardiac monitoring. It was the most demanding role in the nursing team, but Amy Brooks revelled in the different challenges every critically ill or injured patient provided.

Amy even welcomed the apparent initial chaos of receiving and transferring such a patient. Ambulance crew, consultants, registrars, nurses and technical staff all tackling their own tasks within the set protocols. So much happening and so much information being gathered and passed. It took a special ability to be able to assimilate the details, to focus on each task and to switch focus with speed should the situation dictate a new urgency.

'This is Daniel Lever. He's nineteen years old.' The ambulance officer was reinforcing information they had previously radioed through to the department. Transmission was often patchy. 'Car versus truck. Daniel was the single occupant of the car.'

The stretcher was positioned alongside the bed.

'High-speed impact with vehicle rollover.'

Amy noted the cervical collar around the young man's neck and the backboard he was strapped onto. Spinal injuries had to be high on the index of suspicion after the description of the accident.

'Daniel was trapped in the car for approximately forty-five minutes.' The ambulance officer shifted the portable cardiac monitor out of the way. 'Are we ready? One, two…three!'

Amy moved to help lift the backboard. Entrapment time had already eaten well into the 'golden hour'.

'Systolic BP of 90, heart rate 125, respiration rate of 30. Daniel has remained conscious but confused with a GCS of 13. He has chest injuries, including a flail segment with possible pneumothorax, abdominal tenderness and a compound fracture of the left femur.'

Jennifer Bowman was the airway nurse on the team. She was first into action as their patient was transferred to the bed.

'Hello, Daniel. Can you open your eyes for me?' Jennifer disconnected the portable oxygen cylinder and reattached the line to the wall outlet as Daniel groaned in response. She adjusted the position of the high-concentration oxygen mask he was wearing. Amy used shears to clip away the remnants of clothing on Daniel's chest. She glanced at the other nurse as she heard the encouraging murmur of her voice soothing their distressed patient. Jennifer was also responsible for talking to the patient and giving support. The rapport she could establish quickly with people was a strength that Amy appreciated more than most. Jennifer was perfect for the job.

Gareth Harvey, the senior emergency consultant, listened to Daniel's chest with a stethoscope while still receiving information from the ambulance crew.

'He's received 1.5 litres of saline so far. He's also had 10 mg of morphine. Cardiac rhythm's been stable.'

Amy attached the leads for the department's cardiac monitor. Now she wrapped the automatic blood-pressure cuff around Daniel's arm and clipped an oxygen saturation probe over his index finger. They had been unable to get an accurate reading in the ambulance. Judging from Daniel's colour, it wasn't going to indicate a good level of circulating oxygen in his bloodstream. A junior nurse, Janice Healey, was struggling to cut away the denim of Daniel's jeans. He groaned loudly as she tried to pull some fabric clear of the splint on his left leg.

'Leave that for the moment, Janice,' Amy advised. 'And don't take the dressing off the wound until a doctor is ready to look at it. The more exposure it gets, the more likely it is to get contaminated.'

Jennifer was still trying to establish communication. 'Do you know where you are at the moment, Daniel?'

'Can't…breathe…' Daniel gasped. 'Help…me.'

Amy glanced at the monitor. Oxygen saturation was well below ninety per cent. She was reaching for the chest-drain pack before Gareth Harvey requested it. Their patient was desperate to sit up to try and ease his breathing difficulty. Being strapped to a backboard due to the possibility of spinal damage was increasing his distress.

'Left-sided tension pneumothorax,' Gareth informed Amy.

Amy was already drawing up the local anaesthetic. A chest drain had to be inserted as the first priority. Air had entered Daniel's chest outside the lung, probably because of laceration from the broken ribs. The pressure had collapsed the lung and was now threatening the function of the other lung and his heart.

Jennifer had her head bent close to Daniel's. 'We're going to do something to help with your breathing, Daniel,' she told him clearly. 'You might feel a bit of stinging. That's some local anaesthetic going into the side of your chest.'

'BP's dropping,' Amy warned Gareth. 'Systolic's down to 80 and we're getting a few ectopics.' She kept an eye on the irregular beats showing up on the cardiac monitor as she ripped open sterile packs and assisted the consultant to insert the chest drain.

Daniel's breathing improved dramatically as the internal pressure of air was relieved but his blood pressure was still dropping. The registrar who had been busy assessing the abdominal and leg injuries looked worried. He directed Gareth's attention to the abdominal distension that was becoming obvious. Amy changed the bag of IV fluid as the level dropped. The registrar was directed to put in a second IV line and start running Haemaccel instead of saline. Amy ripped open more sterile packs.

The team member responsible for documenting the resuscitation attempt was Peter Milne, one of the department's nurse managers. Amy showed him the empty bag of saline.

'That's the third one so far.' She glanced at the large preprinted form Peter was filling in. 'Oxygen saturation's come up to ninety-three per cent,' she told him. 'BP's dropped to 75.'

Janice Healey was ferrying blood samples. She came back with a distraught-looking middle-aged woman beside her.

'This is Daniel's mother,' she told the team nervously. 'Is it OK if she comes in?'

The registrar had just exposed the open fracture of Daniel's leg for assessment. Daniel's mother lost all the colour from her face. Amy moved to help the woman but Peter beat her to it. He supported her with a firm hand on her arm.

'Janice, take Daniel's mother down to the relatives' room for the moment and stay with her. I'll come down as soon as we have all the information we need to give her the full picture.'

Janice stepped away. 'Come with me, Mrs Lever,' she said hesitantly. Daniel's mother remained glued to the spot, her terrified gaze fixed on her son. Peter raised an eyebrow at Amy, who nodded. She would take over

documenting the case until Peter had settled Mrs Lever
somewhere a little less traumatic. Amy was confident
she could remember the details and be able to record
them during the lull coming up when X-rays would be
taken. It took another twenty minutes until the team
were satisfied that their patient was stable enough to
transfer to Theatre. Surgery was certainly the next priority. The cause of the abdominal bleeding had to be
found and treated if Daniel was going to survive.

'Orthopaedics might want a look at that leg at the
same time,' the registrar suggested. 'Limb baselines are
all well down.'

At the mention of the orthopaedic department
Jennifer caught Amy's eye and winked. Amy ignored
the gesture but was immediately reminded of the knot
of tension she had been harbouring all morning. Not
that she could do anything about it right now. The
trauma case had added to an already busy shift. Amy
had two other patients she needed to go back to monitoring.

The adrenaline rush of working on Daniel's emergency admission wore off only too quickly and Amy
was left feeling strangely nervous. The soft peal of
laughter she heard only minutes later made her turn
swiftly. She couldn't see anything, of course. The curtain around cubicle 4, which she had entered to check
on the elderly Mrs Benny, screened the rest of the department from view. Amy waited several seconds but
couldn't resist the urge to peer around the edge of the
curtain as the sound was repeated. For some peculiar
reason the quiet adult laughter had all the subtlety of
a child's gleeful squeal as far as Amy was concerned.

It wasn't difficult to pinpoint the source of the sound.
The man was still grinning as he straightened up from

leaning on the sorting-desk counter. The unexpected speed with which his gaze shifted from the staff member he'd been in conversation with was unfortunately too sudden to allow Amy's curiosity to remain undetected.

Amy felt the contact as their lines of vision coincided. Their gazes held only for a split second but it was quite long enough for the stranger's mouth to soften and then to begin another curve into a new smile. A smile that was obviously intended for Amy Brooks. Amy whisked the curtain closed hurriedly, turning back to her patient as she cursed her inability to resist peeking. Mrs Benny appeared to be asleep and Amy took the opportunity both to assess her patient and calm herself.

She still felt unnerved. As though the gaze that had caught her own was still there, burning through the thin fabric of the curtain. With a deliberate effort, Amy turned her attention to the fob watch she wore pinned to her uniform. She counted Mrs Benny's rate of breathing, consciously taking several deep breaths herself. It wasn't the stranger's fault she felt rattled. Neither could it be attributed to her current patient. Thanks to the heavy frost that morning, Gladys Benny was the third case of a fractured neck of femur to come through the doors of Queen Mary Hospital's Emergency Department. Straightforward cases with no hint of the drama that had surrounded young Daniel Lever's admission. As common and easy to deal with as the alcohol overdose case Amy was also responsible for in cubicle 2.

The sudden movement of the curtain behind Amy made her jump. The orderly, Derek, grinned widely.

'Gave you a fright, didn't I?' he observed. 'Who did you think I was?'

Amy smiled but ignored the query. She also resisted the urge to look over Derek's shoulder to see who might be standing at the counter being amused by Laura, the sorting-desk clerk. She stifled the slight sense of annoyance that anybody could find being in an emergency department amusing, but her sense of disquiet couldn't be displaced so easily onto some stranger or his laughter. Amy had no one to blame except herself. Her nerves were due to the fact that she was rapidly running out of time. And it wasn't at all funny. Amy touched her patient's hand gently.

'Mrs Benny? Derek is here to take you up to X-ray. How's the pain at the moment?'

Gladys Benny opened her eyes and smiled faintly. 'Much better, thank you, dear. That injection you gave me did the trick nicely. I think I even fell asleep.'

'That's good. We'll see you again as soon as you get back from X-ray.' Amy stood aside as Derek began pushing the bed clear of the cubicle, but Mrs Benny caught hold of Amy's hand and halted the progress.

'What's going to happen to me?' she queried anxiously.

Amy squeezed the frail hand gently. 'It seems likely that you've broken your hip, Mrs Benny. If the X-rays confirm that, then you're going to need an operation, I'm afraid.'

'Oh, dear.' Faded blue eyes filled with tears and the old woman's voice wobbled. 'Where are they going to take me?'

'To X-ray,' Amy reminded her patiently. 'Then you'll come back here and we'll ask the orthopaedic doctors to come and see you. If you do need an operation, we'll arrange admission to one of the wards.'

'So I'm coming back here?' The watery gaze fixed on Amy begged for reassurance.

'Yes, you are, Mrs Benny.' Amy smiled. 'And your daughter's on her way in. I expect she'll be here by the time you get back.'

Amy watched the bed as it was manoeuvred between the sorting-desk counter and an empty ambulance stretcher. Her gaze continued a sweep around the emergency department. The stranger had vanished. Several cubicles and a resus area were empty and the atmosphere was relaxed, with several staff members heading towards the staffroom for a quick break. Jennifer Bowman was amongst the group, in animated conversation with a junior doctor. Amy smiled to herself at the play of expression on her colleague's face.

Jennifer was naturally lively. Gregarious, outspoken—even outrageous at times. To a casual observer, she couldn't have provided much more of a contrast to Amy. It often surprised people to find that the two young women were flatmates, let alone the closest of friends. Amy's inward smile faded and she sighed audibly. It was now past lunchtime on Friday and she was still no closer to the goal she'd set herself a week ago. The pursuit of that goal would have to be postponed yet again if the noises emanating from cubicle 2 were anything to go by.

Amy donned gloves and collected some towels, one of which she dampened at the washbasin. She used the moist towel to clean the face of her patient in cubicle 2.

'Are you feeling better now, Patrick?'

'Aye.' Bleary, bloodshot eyes regarded Amy and

then focused to produce a hint of a familiar twinkle. 'You're an angel, so you are, Amy Brooks.'

'Mmm.' Amy shook her head as she smiled. Patrick Moore was a regular customer, a lonely old Irishman who collected his pension on a Thursday and was often brought into Emergency on a Friday morning, having been discovered hypothermic and drunk in a public park. Unlike many similar patients, Patrick was always grateful for the attention he received and he had a charm that even excessive alcohol abuse couldn't obliterate.

'An angel,' Patrick repeated fervently. 'You've even got a halo.' The old man's expression was so reverent that Amy wondered if he might be experiencing visual disturbances. She held up one hand.

'How many fingers can you see, Patrick?'

'Three,' he told her promptly. 'And beautiful fingers they are, too. Long and dainty—just like the rest of you.' Patrick hiccuped softly and returned his gaze to her head. 'An angel of mercy,' he whispered contentedly. 'With a beautiful golden halo.'

Amy's hand went to her head despite herself. Then she chuckled. 'It's just my hair, Patrick.'

Patrick shook his head and closed his eyes. 'Your hair's all tied up in that fancy knot. It's even speared with that little stick. And it's dark, not shiny and golden. I know a halo when I see one, lassie.'

Amy folded back the blanket covering her patient. There wasn't much point in explaining to Patrick that she'd run out of the hairspray that normally controlled the wispy short tendrils currently escaping her neat hairstyle, and that because it was new growth it was much blonder than the rest of her hair. Or the fact that standing in front of the light source in the cubicle had highlighted the effect. If Patrick wanted to think of her as an angel then that was OK with her.

'It's time to go home again, Patrick,' Amy announced. Mrs Benny would be back from X-ray soon and the increase in general activity and noise beyond the cubicle curtain indicated that the quiet spell was over. Amy helped Patrick to his feet where he stood for a moment, swaying slightly. She pulled back the curtain, glancing up automatically as she did so.

It seemed as though the stranger had been waiting for her to appear. How else could she have caught his eye so instantly? He wasn't laughing this time. Not even smiling, but Amy recognised him. She tore her gaze away. It was like a physical touch, that eye contact. It was too personal. Intimate, even, which was ridiculous. Amy made eye contact with perfect strangers all the time. Why on earth should this man be any different?

'Come on, Patrick. You're all right now.'

Amy turned so that she was side on to the stranger. He was talking to Noel Fenton, an orthopaedic registrar who was probably on his way to see Mrs Benny. Could the man be a relative perhaps? Mrs Benny's son? Amy shook her head unconsciously. No. Mrs Benny was in her eighties and this man didn't look much over thirty. A grandson, maybe.

Amy waited patiently while Patrick collected his hat and walking stick from the end of his bed. She was quite aware of the men in her peripheral line of vision, however. Noel was introducing the man to Gareth Harvey. Amy risked another glance as he shook hands with the consultant. He was smiling again now. His manner was as relaxed and casual as his faded jeans and the leather jacket over an open-necked shirt. Not a frantically worried relative, then.

Amy turned away quickly as the trio of men started moving towards her. Her movement coincided with Patrick's tentative foray back into the world, and the old man staggered a little. He caught Amy's arm and then hooked her waist with a bony hand.

'You're an angel, Amy Brooks,' he proclaimed loudly. 'I love you. Will you marry me?'

Amy prised the hand from her waist. 'Come on, Patrick.' She could sense the proximity of the consultant and his companions. She heard the appreciative chuckle that could only have come from one person. Amy gritted her teeth and spoke with quiet desperation.

'Come *on*, Patrick.' Amy kept hold of her charge's arm and began to steer him very firmly towards the door. Patrick was looking back over his shoulder.

'Sent by heaven, she was,' he informed the department triumphantly. 'An angel, to be sure.'

Amy's blush had finally receded by the time she had signed Patrick out and seen him to the taxi stand outside the waiting room. The nurse manager, Peter Milne, signalled to her on her return.

'Can you give Jennifer a hand to sort out Resus 1? It's still a bit of a mess.'

'Sure.' Amy smiled willingly. 'Any word on Daniel yet?'

'Still in Theatre, but Noel was in there to check on the leg and things were going pretty well. The bleeding's under control. Ruptured spleen and some liver damage. I think he'll pull through.'

'That's great.' Amy spared a thought for the relief Daniel's mother would feel. Jennifer had the same thought when Amy relayed the information.

'Can you believe Janice brought her in here at that point in time? You'd think she'd know enough to check first.'

'I think she feels uncomfortable dealing with relatives,' Amy said. 'And sometimes it is better to let them see that everything possible is being done, especially if the outcome is likely to be bad.'

'Hmm.' Jennifer was counting empty drug ampoules as she slotted them into the sharps container. She didn't sound convinced.

Amy began collecting the discarded sterile packaging. 'Patrick just proposed to me again.'

'So we heard.' Jennifer grinned. 'You're an angel, to be sure.'

Amy returned the grin. Suddenly the moment she'd been waiting for seemed to present itself. 'Hey, Jen?'

'Mmm?' Jennifer was now peering into the drugs cabinet.

'About tonight,' Amy said carefully. She didn't want this opportunity to go the way all the others had. 'I thought—'

'No,' Jennifer interrupted firmly. She kept her gaze on the contents of the cupboard. 'We're low on adrenaline in here. Pretty low on morphine as well. I'll go and get some more.'

'Please, Jen,' Amy said forlornly. 'I really want you to come to this party.'

'No. Sorry, Amy, but I'm not going to change my mind.'

'But you love parties.'

'Not this one I don't. I'd rather stay home and stick needles in my eyes.' Jennifer glanced at Amy. 'Which reminds me. How are those IV cannula supplies?'

'Down on 14-gauge,' Amy responded automatically.

'I'll get some of those, too, then.'

Amy straightened the ECG electrode wires and rolled up the blood-pressure cuff. She was tucking in the clean sheet on the bed as Jennifer returned. Amy accepted the bundle of cannula packages and caught her friend's eye hopefully.

'It won't be that bad, you know. The party, I mean.'

'Yes, it will.' Jennifer was arranging the fresh supply of ampoules in the drug cabinet. 'A pack of stuffy consultants and their wives. All geriatric,' she continued decisively. 'There'll probably be a string quartet in the corner and a waiter with a tray of sherry. Everybody will be overdressed and horribly superior.' Jennifer clicked the cabinet door shut and locked it. She gave Amy a reproachful look. 'And your boyfriend will be the worst of the lot.'

Amy sighed. This wasn't going the way she'd planned it at all. 'Don't start on Nigel,' she begged. 'He's not that bad. He really wants you to come.'

'Oh, sure.' Jennifer's expression was now openly sceptical. You're talking about the man who told me, only yesterday, that if my neurons could get close enough to hold hands occasionally then I would have had those scan results available *before* he had to disrupt his precious schedule to come down to Emergency.'

Amy's glance slid sideways. 'OK, so he can be a bit sarcastic sometimes. Major trauma cases can be stressful, as you well know.'

'He hadn't even got anywhere near the patient,' Jennifer countered. Her expression softened. 'I admit he probably has his good points. He can be very charming when he wants to be.' It was Jennifer's turn to sigh. 'I just can't pretend to like him, Amy. There's something about him that I don't trust, and it's more than the fact that his eyes are far too close together. I still don't understand why you started going out with him in the first place.'

'He asked me,' Amy said simply. 'Anyway, that's months ago, now. It's ancient history.'

'Like Nigel.'

'He's only forty-two,' Amy said impatiently. 'And he's a very talented surgeon. You don't *have* to like him, Jen. Just come to the party. For me.'

'No way.' Jenny pulled back the curtain. Resus 1 was ready to go again. 'Catch you later, Amy. Looks like there's some work to be done out here.'

A new stretcher was coming through the automatic double doors from the ambulance bay. The bed arriving from the other end of the corridor that led into the hospital was returning Mrs Benny to the emergency department. Amy caught up with her patient.

'That was nice and quick. How are you feeling, Mrs Benny?'

'Dreadful. They moved my leg and the pain is ever so much worse.'

'Is is?' Amy helped the orderly position the bed back in cubicle 4. 'I'll get one of the doctors to come and organise some more pain relief for you.'

Amy's route to notify one of the registrars of Mrs Benny's need for more analgesia took her past Jennifer, who was helping a woman towards the toilet. The smile that the two nurses exchanged was fleeting but it was enough to reassure Amy that Jennifer was not really bothered by her persistent efforts over the last week directed at getting her to accept the party invitation.

The difference of opinion concerning Amy's dating of orthopaedic surgeon Nigel Wesley hadn't been enough to seriously compromise their friendship. Yet. Amy's spirits sank a little further. That was something that could well change after tonight, and Amy dreaded that possibility. Somehow she had to warn Jennifer of developments and ensure that their friendship wasn't going to suffer irreparably. Persuading her to attend the party and then making sure she enjoyed herself was the only plan Amy had, so far, been able to concoct.

Perhaps she should just come straight out with it and tell Jennifer the truth. If she was really confident that she was doing the right thing, then it shouldn't be a problem, but confidence was an emotion that Amy generally associated only with her professional abilities. Anything else was too risky to be confident about, but this was a risk she was happy enough to take. It was the right thing to do. It *had* to be. Time was running out in more ways than one.

Maybe the doubts that were troubling her were due to the sneaking suspicion that a friendship might have to be sacrificed. Not just any friendship either. The one and only really close relationship that Amy had ever had with another person. Nobody else had ever come close. Not her school friends and definitely not her parents. Not even Nigel. Maybe especially Nigel. Jen was the one person in the world who loved Amy for who she really was. Jen made her feel good about herself and had always supported her wholeheartedly. Well, almost always. At least until Nigel Wesley had surprisingly shown an interest in Senior Nurse Amy Brooks.

Gladys Benny was transferred to a ward half an hour later. Due to her patient's reluctance to let go of her hand, Amy accompanied the bed as far as the lift. It was on her return that she spotted the man for the third

time. He was now in the emergency observation area—
a mini-ward, adjacent to Emergency, that could hold
non-urgent patients for up to twenty-four hours until a
decision was made regarding their need for admission.
Amy didn't give him the chance to look in her direction
this time. She sped on and didn't stop until she found
Jennifer. She followed her friend into the sluice room.

'Who *is* that man in the leather jacket?' Amy demanded. 'He's been hanging around Emergency all
day.'

'So have I,' Jennifer groaned. She dropped the container she was carrying into the infectious waste disposal unit and stripped off her gloves. 'My feet hurt.'
She gave Amy a concerned glance. 'How's your leg?'

'Fine.' Amy wasn't going to be distracted. 'You
must have noticed him,' she persisted.

'Why? Is he cute?'

'I suppose,' Amy admitted grudgingly. 'He's tall
with straight black hair. Kind of spiky.' She eyed
Jennifer's tufts of short blonde hair. 'A bit like yours,
only longer.'

'I like him already,' Jennifer declared. 'Who's he in
here to see?'

'That's what I was trying to find out.' Amy shook
her head. 'He looks too happy to be a relative.'

'If he looks happy, he can't be a staff member either.' Jennifer grinned.

'I'm not sure about that. Noel Fenton was introducing him to Gareth a while ago.'

'What?' Jennifer's jaw slackened. 'You mean Noel
Fenton was here and I didn't notice?' Her face screwed
itself into total dismay. 'Damn it! That probably means
he didn't notice me either.'

Amy looked suddenly thoughtful. 'Noel is Nigel's registrar.'

'I know that.' Jennifer leaned back against the wall, clearly grateful for a short respite. 'Just because Noel is indescribably gorgeous doesn't make Nigel suitable, however. You could do so much better for yourself, Amy.'

'I haven't so far.' Amy lost her train of thought regarding Noel Fenton. 'I'm nearly thirty, Jen.'

'So? You're gorgeous. Far too good for Mr Wesley.' She nudged Amy. 'You might have hazel eyes instead of blue but, as Patrick says, you're an angel, to be sure.'

Amy laughed. 'If I'm so terrific, how come all my romances have been such dismal failures?' she countered.

'You just haven't found the right man.'

Amy took a deep breath. 'Maybe I have now.'

'Ha!' Jennifer shook her head vigorously. 'For God's sake, Amy. Nigel Wesley still lives with his *mother*!'

'It's a huge house. She has a completely self-contained wing. They lead totally separate lives.'

Jennifer eyed her dubiously.

'The house is awesome, Jen. You really should come and see it. There's an indoor swimming pool and a conservatory. Six bedrooms and all of them have *en suite* bathrooms.'

'You sound like a real estate agent.'

'The garden's well worth seeing. It got photographed for *House and Garden* last year.'

'It'll be dark.'

'It's floodlit,' Amy told her enthusiastically. 'And the kitchen's amazing. All stainless steel and very high tech.'

'Sounds like an operating theatre.' Jennifer giggled. 'Does the food come out on a tray covered with a sterile drape?'

'There's a breakfast room that leads into the conservatory. It has cane furniture and lots of bright cushions. It's really rather nice.'

'You sound like you're planning to move in.'

Amy's hesitation was just long enough for Jennifer's eyes to widen in a horrified expression. 'This party that you're so keen to drag me along to tonight. You're not...' Jennifer swallowed deliberately. 'It's not for some special announcement, is it?'

'Please, come, Jen.' Amy bit her lip. 'I need you there. I need someone on my side.'

'If it feels like a battle then it's not right. Don't do it, Amy.'

'I'm not talking about Nigel. It's the rest of them I'm not so sure of. And I don't think his mother really likes me.' Desperation planted a last ray of hope for Amy as she remembered her earlier inspiration. 'Hey, Jen? What if I got Nigel to invite Noel Fenton to the party?'

'He'd probably bring his wife.'

'I don't think he's married. In fact, I'm sure he isn't. You could wear something gorgeous and he'd have to notice you. You'd stand out a mile amongst all those consultants' wives.' Amy had noticed the gleam of interest her friend was trying to disguise. 'I can see it now,' she said cunningly. 'There they all are. Middle-aged and dressed in sophisticated but terribly boring black evening dresses. And there you are—wearing something—'

'Black,' Jennifer supplied. She grinned at Amy's frown. 'But black with a difference.' She straightened and headed for the door. 'I like it,' she announced. 'I think I will come to your party after all.'

Amy breathed an inward sigh of relief. A bit of moral support was all she needed to make the evening perfect.

'You know…' Jennifer had paused in the sluice room doorway to glance back at Amy. 'I think tonight might just be a turning point in life.'

Amy nodded happily. 'For both of us.' She was still smiling as Jennifer disappeared. It was certainly going to be the turning point of her own life.

Amy Brooks had no doubt at all about that.

CHAPTER TWO

THE nudge from Jennifer Bowman's elbow was none too gentle.

'What is *that*, might I ask?'

Amy's smile was embarrassed. 'It's a string quartet,' she admitted.

'And *where* is it?'

'In the conservatory.'

'And where is Noel?' Jennifer asked pointedly.

'I'm not sure.' Amy cast a hopeful glance at the new faces appearing in the crowded drawing room. 'He'll be here very soon, I expect.'

'He'd better be,' Jennifer muttered darkly. She, too, glanced at the gathering of people. 'This is even worse than I expected. Look—half of them are drinking sherry.'

'I see you found the champagne, though.'

'Of course. Where's yours?'

'I finished it already.' Amy bit her lip. 'I think I was a bit nervous.'

'So? Have another one.' Jennifer signalled a waiter who arrived at her side bearing a tray of crystal flutes, the pale gold liquid they contained fizzing discreetly. Jen winked at Amy. 'I could get used to this. I'm even beginning to understand the attraction of Nigel Wesley.'

'Shh. You promised you wouldn't say anything.' Amy took a sip from her glass. 'I'm supposed to be in the foyer with Nigel, greeting the new arrivals. He'll be wondering why I'm taking so long in the bathroom.'

'Let him wonder,' Jennifer advised. 'Every woman needs a mystery or two.'

'Where did you disappear to when I *was* in the bathroom?'

'I was checking out the conservatory.' Jennifer waved vaguely behind her then grinned at Amy. 'You'll never believe this, but I met a vampire.'

'Oh, sure.' Amy took another sip of champagne. Thank goodness Jen had agreed to come to this party. She could almost pretend she was enjoying herself despite the fact that they were being largely ignored by the people around them.

'I'm not kidding. There was this tall, tall woman with dead white skin and jet black hair, all scraped back into a net thing. She had blood red lips and matching nails.'

Amy couldn't stifle her smile. 'I think you just met Lorraine.'

'Who's Lorraine?'

'Nigel's mother.'

'No!' Jen breathed. 'How old is she?'

'I don't know. Must be in her sixties, I guess.'

Jen looked thoughtful. 'Maybe scraping your hair back tightly enough has the same effect as a face lift. She doesn't look that old.' Jennifer leaned closer to Amy. 'Then again,' she whispered, 'being unable to go out in daylight might work quite well, too.'

Amy giggled with genuine amusement but the pleasure died swiftly as the subject of their conversation appeared beside her.

'I'm delighted to see you enjoying yourself, Amy.' Lorraine Wesley didn't look particularly delighted. Her gaze swept over Jennifer briefly with an ill-concealed flicker of distaste. Amy's hackles rose. Jennifer might have overdone things just a little, with her black mini-skirt, tight-fitting top and the number of earrings she had chosen to wear, but she looked stunning in Amy's opinion. She had always envied her friend's figure.

Maybe Lorraine Wesley was envious as well. The elegant black sheath dress her prospective mother-in-law was wearing revealed a body lacking any feminine curves. Lorraine's sharp glance landed on Amy again.

'Shouldn't you be with Nigel at the moment?'

'I'm on my way, Mrs Wesley,' Amy said quickly. 'Have you met my friend, Jennifer?'

'Ah!' Lorraine Wesley made it sound as though a mystery had been finally solved. She nodded with deliberate graciousness at Jennifer.

'Jen's my flatmate,' Amy said defensively. 'It's thanks to her I had something to wear tonight. She lent me her ballgown.' She smoothed a nervous hand over the full skirt of the floor-length, midnight blue gown.

'Ah!' Lorraine repeated meaningfully. 'No wonder the bodice looks a little big for you, my dear.' Sculptured eyebrows creased a fraction. 'What have you got on your feet?'

Amy didn't dare look at Jen's expression. She took a long swallow of her champagne before poking her foot further out from the folds of the dress. 'What's wrong with my shoes?'

'Nothing at all, dear,' Lorraine assured her. 'Except they're *flat*. One should never wear flat shoes with evening dress.' Lorraine Wesley laughed tolerantly. 'In fact, one should probably avoid wearing flat shoes at any time.' The older woman was turning away as she spoke. 'Ah, Rodney! How fabulous to see you again.'

'I should have told her I have flat feet,' Amy muttered rebelliously. 'And I need the shoes to match.'

Jennifer was looking unusually serious. 'Doesn't she know *why* you wear flat shoes?'

'Of course not.' Amy looked uncomfortable. 'I'd better go and find Nigel. Excuse me.'

'No, you don't.' Jennifer was following her. 'I want to know something, Amy Brooks.'

'What?' Amy stopped near the string quartet. The music covered their voices.

'Has Nigel ever tried to take you dancing on one of these weekly dates you've been having?'

'No. We usually have dinner or go to a concert or movie. Or both. You know that.'

'Has he ever seen you in a short skirt?'

'Do I ever wear short skirts?' Amy countered.

'Exactly.' Jennifer lowered her voice. 'Have you slept with Nigel Wesley, Amy?'

'Jen!' Amy looked quickly over her shoulder.

'*Have* you?' Jen persisted.

'Not exactly,' Amy admitted reluctantly.

Jennifer sighed with exasperation. 'Amy, how could you even *think* of marrying a man who doesn't even know about something that significant in your life?'

'He knows about my leg,' Amy muttered. 'He just hasn't *seen* it. It's not that significant, anyway. Or it shouldn't be.'

'But it is,' Jennifer contradicted. 'You know it is, Amy. It was the reason you broke up with what's-his-name—that chap you were almost engaged to before you moved to Christchurch.' Jennifer sounded desperate. 'Amy, you *can't* marry Nigel Wesley.'

'Yes, I can,' Amy said quietly. 'It's my choice. He asked me and I said yes.'

'But *why*?' Jennifer wailed softly.

'Because I want a family,' Amy said sincerely. 'I want children. So does Nigel. He'll be a good father. He takes his responsibilities very seriously.'

'That's not enough,' Jen told her.

'He loves me,' Amy said firmly. 'And I love him.'

'Do you?' Jennifer's mouth twisted doubtfully. 'Do you *really* love him?'

'I think so,' Amy replied. 'Who really knows for sure?'

'I would,' Jennifer said with conviction. 'And so should you. This isn't good enough.'

'It's all that's on offer.' Amy drained her glass and set it down on a side table. 'And I'm not going to lose the only chance I might ever get.' She could see Nigel approaching. So could Jen.

'He looks just like his mother,' Jennifer observed casually. 'Except she hasn't got the beard...yet.'

Amy had to smile, she couldn't help herself. Nigel was tall, slim and dark like his mother. His hair was swept back to sit neatly on his head. Everything about Nigel was neat. His black dinner suit fitted perfectly. The bow tie sat perfectly straight. His beard and moustache were trimmed with military precision. The impression of intolerance to anything stepping out of line was undermined only by the charming smile he directed at Amy.

'I thought I'd lost you, darling,' he said. 'Come on. There's someone I really want to introduce you to. Stuart Latimer is visiting from London.' He linked Amy's arm through his, gave Jennifer an apologetic inclination of his head and pulled Amy away. 'You haven't got a drink yet,' he observed in surprise. 'Let me find you a glass of champagne.'

Stuart Latimer was a large man, currently in conversation with Lorraine Wesley. He was clearly very impressed by the canapés being offered. One hand was covered by a serviette on which several small savouries nestled.

'Delicious,' he explained to Amy after they had been introduced. 'Never tasted anything so good.'

'They're not too bad, are they?' Lorraine looked satisfied. 'I expect we'll use these caterers for the wedding.'

'When's that going to be?' Stuart enquired. He winked at Amy. 'You're a lucky girl, aren't you?'

'Oh, I'm the lucky one, Stuart,' Nigel put in quickly. He slid an arm around Amy's waist, which reminded her of her encounter with Patrick Moore earlier that day. She took a gulp of champagne.

'October, we thought.' Lorraine was eager to respond to Stuart's question. 'In a month or so.'

'Did we?' Amy was startled.

'In the garden,' Lorraine added.

'Really?' Amy twisted to look at Nigel. 'I don't remember discussing this.'

Nigel and Lorraine exchanged a glance. 'We're getting ahead of ourselves,' Lorraine apologised. 'After all, we haven't even announced the engagement.'

'Any chance of some more nibbles?'

'Of course, Stuart.' Lorraine looked relieved. 'Come with me and we'll find someone to look after you.'

Nigel steered Amy towards another knot of people. 'I haven't told you how gorgeous you're looking tonight. Just perfect. You must wear your hair loose like that more often.'

'I've got flat shoes,' Amy confessed.

'Of course you do. High heels wouldn't be very practical for you, would they?'

'Your mother thinks flat shoes should never be worn.'

Nigel smiled. 'Don't listen to my mother.' He bent his head close to Amy's. 'She can be a bit overbearing at times.' Nigel's breath tickled Amy's ear. 'We'll make our own decisions, Amy. You and me.'

Amy took a relieved swallow of her drink. She had nothing to worry about. Nigel could handle his mother. They would choose their own wedding arrangements. She would get married in a church, just to go against Lorraine's wishes. They would have it catered by a restaurant. And Amy would wear completely flat shoes. Amy smiled brilliantly at Nigel before turning to the man beside him.

'You know Murray Brownlie, don't you, Amy?'

'Yes.' Amy's smile was now shy. She had seen the eminent head of general surgery on many occasions but never on a social basis. Amy listened to the rest of the introductions and then caught the surgeon's eye.

'Did you operate on Daniel Lever earlier today?'

'The young man whose car had the argument with a truck?' Murray Brownlie nodded. 'Indeed I did. He was lucky to survive.'

'I hear he needed a splenectomy,' Amy said. 'Was that the main source of the abdominal bleeding?'

'Hard to say whether the spleen or the liver was winning in the blood loss stakes. We ran through twelve units of whole blood before we had things finally sorted. We used autologous blood as well.'

'That's where you collect the patient's own blood and give it back to them, isn't it?' Amy asked with interest.

The surgeon nodded. 'You aspirate clean blood from the abdomen, anticoagulate it and return it to the patient via an IV cannula with a "cell saver" system.'

'I've never seen it used,' Amy confessed. 'Daniel must have had some massive bleeding going on.'

'One of the biggest liver lacerations I've tackled in quite a while, actually.' Murray Brownlie glanced over his shoulder and then gave Amy the ghost of a wink as he lowered his voice. 'My wife hates me talking shop,' he told her. 'Whereas I simply can't resist.' He smiled broadly. 'Anyway, we sutured and ligated all the bleeding points we could find on young Daniel's liver and then drained it all, but we still couldn't get control. It was rather frustrating.'

'What did you do?' Amy was listening avidly.

'Well, we achieved temporary control by clamping the free edge of the lesser omentum.' Murray eyed Amy cautiously. 'Does that mean anything to you?'

Amy nodded. 'The omentum is a fold of the peritoneum that extends from the stomach to adjacent abdominal organs. The lesser omentum connects to the liver.'

The surgeon looked impressed. 'Precisely. We considered putting in an omental pack and suturing it in place, but it wasn't going to work so we ended up doing a hepatic lobectomy. Took quite a chunk of the lad's liver out but it's an amazing organ. Young Daniel should be functioning again quite normally in no time.' Murray Brownlie smiled at Amy kindly. 'This really does interest you, doesn't it?'

Amy nodded. 'I love everything about my job. I only wish I could follow the patients up more sometimes.'

'Feel free to come and observe in Theatre any time,'

the surgeon invited. 'Or come and visit the wards on your days off.'

'Oh, I'd love to do that,' Amy said. 'Thank you.' She smiled excitedly at Nigel who had just finished his own conversation. Amy was keenly aware of a feeling of gratitude towards Nigel as well as the head of general surgery. Nigel's respected position at the hospital was opening all sorts of doors for her. It was rather a heady sensation, being taken seriously by someone like Murray Brownlie.

Murray turned to Nigel. 'If this young lady is half as keen on you as she is on her job, then you're a lucky man.'

'I am lucky,' Nigel agreed, smiling. 'But I don't think I need to compete with a job, do I, Amy?'

'Of course not,' Amy said obligingly. She didn't quite follow Nigel's meaning but dismissed the puzzle in favour of sipping her drink. A waiter appeared with a magnum wrapped in a snowy white linen cloth. He topped up her glass as an elegant woman joined them.

'Have you met my wife, Nigel?' Murray enquired. 'This is Helen.'

'Hello Nigel.' Helen smiled. 'I do hope my husband's not being a bore and talking shop. This is a stunning party.'

'Thanks.' Nigel allowed Helen to kiss him on both cheeks.

'I've just heard about Sydney. Congratulations.'

'Thanks,' Nigel said again. He touched Amy's arm. 'I must introduce you to some more people.' He excused them from the Brownlies' group.

'What's happening in Sydney?' Amy asked.

'Chair of Orthopaedic Surgery,' Nigel said proudly.

'It's just been announced.' He smiled at Amy. 'They chose me.'

'I didn't know you'd applied.' Amy stopped, feeling suddenly bewildered.

'I didn't want to disappoint you if I missed out.'

Amy shook her head, trying to clear her thoughts. 'Are you planning to *live* in Sydney?'

'Of course. It's fantastic, isn't it? I was intending to surprise you with the news later.'

'Oh.' Amy felt a wave of dizziness. 'I'm surprised, Nigel.'

'You don't look very excited.'

'Where am I supposed to live, Nigel? While you're living in Sydney?'

Nigel's smile was contrite. 'Oh, I'm sorry, Amy. You didn't think I was planning to leave you behind, did you? I have no intention of going until after the wedding, don't worry. We won't have to be separated for any length of time.'

'And this wedding is going to be in October, right?'

'If that's what you'd like.' Nigel was still smiling, pleased at having sorted out the misunderstanding.

'You mean I get a say in this after all?'

Nigel now looked disconcerted. 'Maybe we should talk about this later, Amy.'

'Maybe we should,' Amy agreed. Maybe it wasn't just Nigel's mother who was autocratic and overbearing. Amy felt confused. There was too much she needed to think about and her brain wasn't functioning nearly as clearly as it had been before that last glass of champagne. 'Excuse me, Nigel, but I really need to go to the bathroom.'

'Again?'

Amy took pleasure in ignoring Nigel's vaguely disapproving tone. She walked out of the drawing room, through the conservatory where she helped herself to a bottle of champagne waiting on the side table. Then she let herself out of the French doors onto a verandah that overlooked the garden. Stepping carefully, Amy negotiated the steps and turned onto a path that she knew led to the summer house.

'What does he expect?' Amy muttered to herself. 'He clicks his fingers and I give up my job and trot off to Sydney?' She paused to drink champagne and top up her glass. 'What am I supposed to be? Robo-Wife?'

Maybe Jennifer was right and she shouldn't marry Nigel. What did he have going for him, apart from being single, successful, usually charming and apparently madly in love with her?

'Oh, hell.' Amy took another mouthful of wine. He had quite a lot going for him, really. Was she going to throw it all away because she felt miffed that Nigel hadn't asked what she'd wanted before letting his mother plan the wedding?

The floodlighting hadn't been turned on at the summer house but the white paintwork was easy enough to see in the dark. A mossy statue to one side of the garden structure was also just visible. A sort of large garden nymph holding garlands of foliage.

'Why is it?' Amy asked the statue, 'that the things that really matter to me don't seem to be important to anyone else?'

To Amy's astonishment, the statue answered her. 'You tell me,' it said.

'It's because I was never quite good enough,' Amy told the statue sadly. 'I was supposed to have been a boy, you know.'

'Really?' The statue seemed very interested.

'Yes.' Amy drained her glass. 'My father never got over the disappointment.'

'Well, he was a bloody idiot, then, wasn't he?' The statue was moving. Amy gasped in horror as the figure stepped from the shadows. Even in this dim light she recognised him. He was still wearing the same faded jeans and leather jacket. Amy's gaze travelled up to meet his. She felt that odd physical buzz again. The only eye contact in existence with the ability to caress. There could be no doubt at all, even in her fuzzy state. It was definitely the same man.

'You've been following me around all day,' Amy said accusingly. 'What the hell are you doing here?'

'I heard there was a party.'

Amy eyed his clothing suspiciously. 'Were you invited, then?'

The man grinned. 'No. I'm gatecrashing.'

Amy narrowed her gaze. 'So why are you out here hiding in the garden, then?'

'I'm still trying to decide whether I want to go in or not.' He stepped closer. 'Do you think I should?'

'No.' Amy tilted the bottle towards her glass. 'It's not much fun.' The slosh of champagne missed her glass and foamed over her hand.

'Here, let me.' The man took the bottle from her hand and held the glass as he filled it. Then he took a long swallow before setting both the bottle and glass down on the white wrought-iron table. Taking a handkerchief from his pocket, he took hold of Amy's hand and wiped it.

'I'm sorry you're not having fun,' he commiserated.

'So am I,' Amy agreed wistfully. She looked at her hand. It was dry now but was still being held. Looking up, she found his gaze fixed firmly on her face. His eyes were brown. A lovely, warm, velvety brown. Comforting but disturbing at the same time. 'Why are you staring at me?'

'You're a very attractive woman.'

'You've been staring at me all day.'

'You've been very attractive all day.'

Amy smiled. He didn't miss a beat. A smooth talker. He was probably very good at kissing, too. Her gaze slid down involuntarily to assess his lips.

'I've been thinking about that myself.'

'About what?' Amy murmured. She wasn't ready to be distracted.

'About this.' Smoothly, he moved closer. Bent his head and touched his lips to hers. And there was Amy Brooks, absent without leave from her own engagement party, kissing a total stranger in the summer house. And she had been right. He was very good. Very, very good. Amy didn't want him to stop. She didn't care about breathing any more. Who needed air when you had *this*?

But he did stop. He drew back from her lips slowly. Maybe he didn't really want to stop either.

'Sent from heaven is right,' he said in awed tones. The soft brown gaze was locked on Amy again. 'You *are* an angel.' He cleared his throat. 'Must be something in the air. I hear that Nigel is announcing his engagement to some poor woman tonight.'

The observation had all the effect of a cold shower. 'He is,' Amy confirmed curtly. 'And I'm the poor woman.'

The man let go of her as if he'd been burnt. He took a step back. 'What the hell were you kissing me for, then?'

'I wasn't,' Amy denied hotly. 'You were kissing me.'

'You let me.'

'So it's all my fault?' Amy queried sweetly. 'Typical!'

'You must be mad,' the man told her.

'Why, because I let you kiss me? I might be inclined to agree with you there, mate.'

'Because you're planning to marry Nigel Wesley.' The gaze, still fixed on Amy, darkened. He actually looked angry. 'What's the attraction?' he asked unpleasantly. 'Money?'

'Of course not,' Amy snapped. 'And it's none of your business.' He wasn't the only one who could get angry. 'Just what gives you the right to express opinions on something you know absolutely nothing about?' Amy snorted incredulously. 'What is it about me? Even a perfect stranger thinks he can tell me what I should or shouldn't be doing.' Amy snatched up the bottle of champagne and her glass.

'Stay out of it,' she ordered imperiously. 'And stop…' She glanced over her shoulder, causing her progress down the path to weave quite dramatically. 'Stop *staring* at me.'

Amy sailed back into the house, through the conservatory towards the drawing room. Jennifer was standing in the breakfast nook near the entrance to the kitchen. A waiter stood beside her holding a large silver tray covered with bite-sized savouries.

'What's in the little round ones?' Jennifer was asking.

'Satay chicken.' The waiter seemed to be enjoying the attention.

'And the triangles?'

'Sun-dried tomatoes, feta cheese and olives.'

'Have you found Noel yet?' Amy asked Jennifer.

'No, but I forgive you anyway, Amy. These things are delicious. Have some satay chicken.'

'I'm not hungry,' Amy stated. She eyed the mass of humanity visible through the double doors of the drawing room. Nigel's face appeared. He frowned at Amy. Amy sighed loudly.

'What's the matter?' Jennifer spoke around a mouthful of filo pastry. She grabbed another savoury from the platter as the waiter moved towards the door. He nearly collided with Nigel.

'Amy, where on earth have you been? Lorraine's waiting to make the announcement.'

'I'm sure she can wait a bit longer,' Amy said evenly. 'Or is it getting a bit close to dawn?'

Jennifer sputtered over the remains of her pastry. Nigel's frown deepened.

'What?' His expression changed to one of calculation. 'How much have you had to drink tonight, Amy?'

'Not much,' Amy lied. 'In fact, I think I'll have some more.' She reached out and collected a full crystal flute from the silver tray another waiter was taking into the gathering. Goodness knows what she'd done with the bottle and glass she'd been holding a few minutes ago.

'I think you've had enough,' Nigel told her.

'Amy's quite capable of deciding when she's had enough to drink,' Jennifer informed Nigel.

'That's right.' Amy nodded. 'To tell the truth, I'm getting a little bit fed up with other people deciding things on my behalf.'

'Good for you, Amy,' Jennifer said encouragingly.

'Yes, good for you,' a voice echoed.

Amy swivelled sharply. There he was again! In the kitchen!

'What the *hell* are you doing here?' Nigel queried coldly.

'That's just what I was going to ask,' Amy said in surprise.

'Shut up, Amy.' Nigel was glaring at the intruder.

'I beg your pardon? You can't speak to me like that, Nigel.'

The man nodded calmly. 'Damned right he can't. You tell him, Amy.'

Jennifer grinned at the stranger. 'I think I like you,' she announced.

The catering staff had all paused in their tasks. They were staring openly at the scene unfolding before them in the breakfast room.

Nigel took hold of Amy's arm. 'Come with me,' he ordered curtly.

'No,' Amy protested but her legs were too wobbly to cooperate. She found herself being pulled across the hallway and into the throng of guests. Her support team had vanished. She was in enemy territory again. Gaps appeared in the crowd as Nigel moved purposefully forward. Greetings and conversational openings were acknowledged merely by a brisk nod from Nigel. Then the progress halted abruptly. Nigel's registrar, Noel Fenton, was standing in front of them.

'Noel,' Amy said happily. 'Jen's been looking for you.'

'Jen? Who's Jen?'

'Never mind,' Nigel snapped. 'Listen, Noel. Amy needs to go home. She's over-indulged a little. Can I leave it to you to—?'

'Jennifer Bowman, my flatmate,' Amy told Noel earnestly. 'She's very keen to meet you and I promised—'

'Amy!' Nigel gave her arm a shake.

Amy jerked away from his hand. 'Don't shake me, Nigel,' she warned sharply. 'And don't tell me to shut up again either.'

Lorraine glided into view. Her voice was deceptively light. 'Goodness me! What *is* going on?'

'I'll tell you,' Amy volunteered. 'Nigel thinks I'm a sort of puppet. He can shake me and I'll do whatever he thinks I should do.'

'Nigel?' Lorraine's tone carried a distinct 'please explain' message. Amy was delighted to see the composure crack.

'Nigel thinks I'm going to live in Sydney,' she told Lorraine. 'He thinks my job doesn't matter a damn and I'll just give it up. Just like that!' Amy tried to click her fingers but the result was unsatisfyingly muted. She tried again.

Lorraine glanced around them. Several nearby people had fallen silent and were pretending not to be watching. She gave an apologetic laugh. 'Really, Amy. I think you might be overreacting.'

'You would think that,' Amy agreed. 'But you're just as bad as he is. You've even got my wedding all planned and you didn't bother talking to me about it, did you?'

More people were listening. The first group had given up any pretence of not being fascinated. They had been joined by Jennifer and the stranger in the leather jacket.

'I have an announcement to make.' Amy took a breath, hoping that the loud buzzing in her head might dissipate. She handed her glass to Noel who looked like he was trying his best not to smile.

'I'm not going to marry you, Nigel,' Amy said loudly. 'I'd rather…' She paused as a wave of dizziness threatened her upright posture.

'Go, Amy!' Jen crowed.

Amy smiled lopsidedly. 'I'd rather go home and stick needles in my eyes,' she told Nigel.

'Definitely preferable,' the stranger agreed. He and Jen exchanged a grin.

'Going home is certainly a good idea,' Nigel said coldly. 'I'll drive you myself.'

'No way!' Amy wagged a finger at Nigel. 'You're not doing anything for me, Nigel Wesley.' She could feel herself swaying. 'You know what I think you should do, Nigel?' Amy didn't wait for a response. Her voice rose triumphantly and she enunciated with dramatic deliberation. 'I think you should marry your *mother*!'

Only Amy seemed to find this funny. The silence in the room was now absolute. Even the string quartet in the conservatory had stopped providing any background music. Jennifer and her companion exchanged another glance. Then the man stepped forward.

'Time to go, Amy,' he suggested firmly.

Before she could make any kind of protest, Amy found herself swept up in the man's arms. He turned and strode out of the room. For the first time Amy became aware of the amount of attention she had drawn to herself. Shocked and disapproving faces seemed to be turned on her from every direction.

'Oh, no!' Amy moaned. She buried her face in the

leather-covered shoulder, wrapping her arms around the man's neck to make her defensive position more secure.

'What *have* I done?'

CHAPTER THREE

AMY BROOKS had ruined her life, that's what she'd done.

It took until Sunday evening for the physical aftermath of the party to abate completely. By then it was only too clear that the emotional damage was irreparable. While Jennifer had been sympathetic enough concerning Amy's physical woes, she was demonstrating a sad lack of empathy for Amy's state of personal anguish. Admittedly, it was fair enough that Jennifer had escaped by working her rostered day shifts on Saturday and Sunday. As far as Amy was concerned, it hadn't been a matter of vital necessity that Jennifer had accepted the date with Noel Fenton on the Saturday night. And she really didn't need to look quite so cheerful as she tackled her pile of ironing on Sunday evening.

'Do you want me to iron a uniform for you as well?'

'I don't need one,' Amy said gloomily. 'I'm not going to work tomorrow.'

'Yes, you are,' Jennifer contradicted. 'You have to help me pay the rent.'

'I'll get another job. I'll become a photographer's assistant and spend my days locked in a darkroom.'

'You love your job.'

'Not any more, I don't. How can I even show my face at work? The entire hospital must be talking about me.'

'Not so far.' Jennifer was pulling a pair of black

tights from the washing basket. 'These are yours,' she announced, rolling them up and throwing them to where Amy was sitting, curled up on the end of the couch. Amy caught the tights and dumped them on the pile of unfolded underwear she was accumulating beside her.

'I've ruined my life,' she said mournfully. 'Nigel will never speak to me again.'

'Every cloud has a silver lining, I guess.' Jennifer was unsympathetic. 'Here, is this your uniform?' She held up a crumpled white smock.

Amy nodded. 'You can have it.'

'It wouldn't fit me. Anyway, you'll need it tomorrow morning.'

'No, I won't. I'll call in sick.'

'I'll tell them,' Jennifer threatened. 'For God's sake, Amy. If people do hear about the party they'll think you're a hero. Nobody really likes Nigel Wesley.' Jennifer spread the uniform over the board. 'Except maybe his mother,' she added thoughtfully. The iron was picked up but then thumped back onto its holder. '*He's* the one who should feel embarrassed. *He's* the one who got dumped.'

'I didn't *dump* him,' Amy wailed. 'It was just a misunderstanding.'

Jennifer began ironing again. 'I suspect that telling Nigel you'd rather stick needles in your eyes than marry him might just have given him the impression he was being dumped,' she suggested wickedly.

Amy groaned.

'Especially when it was done in front of about a hundred people,' Jennifer continued remorselessly.

Amy closed her eyes. Jennifer ironed in silence for a minute and then sighed with what sounded suspiciously like pleasure. Amy cracked one eye open cautiously. Yes, her flatmate was smiling.

'It was really quite romantic, you know. It's a shame you weren't conscious enough to appreciate it.' Jennifer sighed again. 'It was just like that scene in *An Officer And A Gentleman*. You know, the one where he sweeps his girlfriend into his arms and carries her off through all the people in the factory?'

'I'm not his girlfriend. I don't even know the man.'

'Yes, you do,' Jennifer said reproachfully. 'I told you all about him yesterday.' She eased Amy's uniform onto a hanger. 'His name's Tom Barlow and he's our new locum emergency department consultant. He's come from a specialist trauma team in Chicago.' Jennifer hung the uniform from the top of the door. 'Let's hope he doesn't miss all those gunshot and stabbing injuries too much.'

'Let's hope he does,' Amy muttered. 'He might go away again.'

'He grew up here. He wanted to come home.'

'You seem to know an awful lot about him.'

'He was very helpful when Noel was driving us all home from the party. After we'd poured you into bed, we had a coffee. Tom wanted to know all about you.'

'And you *told* him?' Amy squeaked with indignation as she sat bolt upright on the couch for the first time that evening.

'Not everything,' Jennifer said soothingly. 'In fact, not much at all, really. It was more your relationship with Nigel Wesley he was interested in.'

'What relationship?' Amy groaned.

'Exactly. He seemed very pleased that you'd ended it.'

'I haven't ended it,' Amy protested wearily. 'At least, I didn't mean to.'

'Tom said the bit he liked the best was when you told Nigel he should marry his mother.'

'Oh, God,' Amy breathed. 'Did I *really* say that?'

'You did.' Jennifer nodded seriously. 'I was so proud of you. I think Tom was pretty impressed, too. And Noel thought you were great.' Jennifer beamed at Amy. 'It's entirely your doing that Noel has finally noticed me. I'll love you for ever. He said he'd never been to a more memorable party and he's really looking forward to working tomorrow.'

'Why?'

'He said that Nigel Wesley's temper can be bad enough on a good day. He reckons that tomorrow might set a record that will go down in hospital history. He promised to take me out for a drink and tell me all about it.'

'That does it.' Amy closed her eyes again. 'I'm *definitely* not going in to work.'

The emergency department at Queen Mary's looked just the way it always did. Amy could almost imagine that nothing cataclysmic had happened in her life when she arrived to begin her early shift at 6 a.m. the next day. By 9.30 a.m. she was beginning to forget her dread of being there. So far, there had been no terrible reminders of Friday night. Nobody had said anything. The department was busy and Amy was able to throw herself into her work with an almost normal level of enthusiasm.

The department was busy but not stressed. There were three cases of chest pain, a case of pneumonia, a woman with severe abdominal pain, a young man who'd suffered a seizure, some minor injuries from a car accident and a child with possible meningitis.

'It's probably flu,' the registrar told Amy after he'd checked the toddler. 'There's no sign of a rash or any neck stiffness. What's the temperature at the moment?'

'Thirty-nine point nine,' Amy supplied.

'Has she vomited again since she's been here?'

'No. She's pretty miserable, though, and she's been knocking her head on the mattress, so her headache hasn't responded to the paracetamol yet.'

'She's a bit dehydrated, which won't be helping. I think we'll get some fluids into her IV and admit her to the paediatric observation unit, at least for the day. Can you give them a ring? I won't put the IV in until we know we've got a bed available. I'll go and check that chest pain in Resus 2 while you sort that out.'

Amy dodged an incoming stretcher and made for the telephone on the sorting desk. She checked the laminated chart on the wall for the extension number she needed and was about to dial when she felt a touch on her elbow.

'Amy, have you been introduced to Tom Barlow?'

'No,' Amy said truthfully. Even before she turned she could feel that tactile gaze from those brown eyes fixed on her. She directed her gaze towards nurse manager Peter Milne. 'I think I...I saw him around, though,' she stammered. 'On Friday.'

'Tom's going to be heading the resus team when he's on duty.' Peter didn't seem to notice Amy's discomfort. He turned to the man beside him. 'Tom, this is Amy Brooks. She's the circulation nurse on the team.'

Amy had to look at him now. She had to accept the outstretched hand.

'I'm delighted to meet you, Amy,' Tom Barlow said politely. The brown eyes held a disconcertingly amused gleam. 'It's not often I get introduced to a genuine angel.'

Peter looked nonplussed but then grinned. 'Oh, of course. You were here on Friday, when Amy was looking after Patrick.'

Amy pulled her hand free. 'I hope you'll enjoy working here, Dr Barlow,' she managed evenly.

'Call me Tom. And I expect it will be heavenly.' Tom's smile expanded lazily and Peter chuckled.

'Don't expect perfection, Tom. While I have to admit I've never seen Amy behaving badly, I'm sure it's not beyond the realms of possibility.'

'I'm sure it's not.'

Amy could feel the ominous prickle of embarrassed heat assault her neck. Was he referring to the spectacular scene she'd created at the Wesley household which Peter seemed mercifully unaware of? Or was it the fact that she'd kissed a complete stranger—correction, let a complete stranger kiss her, presumably only minutes away from announcing her engagement to another man. If Amy remembered nothing else with vivid clarity from that disastrous evening, she certainly remembered that kiss. The heat had reached more than her cheeks by the time she'd picked up the phone and dialled the extension number.

'Hi,' she said hurriedly. 'It's Amy here, from Emergency.' It felt like tiny flames might erupt from her face at any moment but the men beside her still hadn't moved away. 'We've got a three-year-old girl here who came in query meningitis. She's dehydrated and pyrexic. We'd like to admit her for observation and some fluid replacement, at least short term. Have you got a bed available?'

They were finally moving away. Amy took a deep breath and sighed with relief. She didn't have to look at Tom Barlow again for the moment. With a bit of luck the overpowering internal sensation which the memory of his kiss had again provoked would now fade completely. Amy wished, somewhat desperately, that she never had to look at Tom Barlow again. The memory would be hard enough to banish all on its own.

The music had to be faced some time. Amy might have guessed that the downward slide would begin when Janice Healey came on duty at midday. Start times for shifts in the emergency department were staggered to allow for more continuity of patient care. Jennifer was doing the same shift as Janice today but she'd arrived earlier and was now sitting in the staffroom, sharing Amy's lunch-break.

'I hear it was an interesting party on Friday night, Amy.' Janice was unpacking food supplies from her shoulder-bag.

Amy glanced suspiciously at Jennifer who grimaced ruefully. 'I think Noel might have been entertaining the other registrars a bit yesterday,' she admitted.

Janice flicked her sleek bob as she turned to flash Amy an expression of bemusement laced with satisfaction.

'You must be mad,' she suggested, looking pleased with her analysis of the situation. 'There's no way I'd stuff up an opportunity like that.' Janice shook her head and opened the small fridge.

'You never know, Janice,' Jennifer said kindly, 'you

might just be lucky enough to *get* an opportunity like that one day.'

'Luck has nothing to do with it.' Janice removed someone's lunch-box from the shelf to make room for her supply of yoghurt and fruit. 'I have every intention of being married by the time I'm twenty-five.' She peered at her container of yoghurt. 'There's no way *I'm* going to end up going past my "use by" date.'

'How old *are* you, Janice?' Amy queried.

'Twenty-four. And a half.' Janice smiled knowingly. 'But six months is plenty of time when the right man is available.'

'Nigel Wesley's available,' Jennifer said with a straight face. 'Go for it, Janice.'

'Hmm.' Janice appeared to give the option due consideration. 'Well, he's older and quite successful. And he *is* a doctor, but he doesn't quite make the grade. Unfortunately, I can't stand facial hair.' Janice's shudder was beautifully done.

'What poor victim did you have in mind, then?' Jennifer demanded. Her glance towards Amy suggested that it had better not be Noel Fenton.

'Not telling.' Janice smiled. She shook the wings of black hair away from her face and glanced at the clock. 'Time for work,' she announced cheerfully.

Jennifer scowled at Janice's back as she left. 'Who's she working on? That's what I'd like to know.'

As though in answer to her question, another figure appeared in the staffroom doorway.

'Hi, Tom.' Jennifer's greeting was warm. 'How's the first day going?'

'So far, it's been...' Tom flicked a glance towards Amy and his lips quirked as he repressed a smile '...very nice. Uneventful. Quite manageable, in fact. I almost know where to find everything now.' He reached for a cup and spooned coffee into it. 'How's your day going, Amy?'

'Fine, thanks.' Amy was hurriedly tidying up the remnants of her lunch.

'No Resus Team calls yet.' Tom sounded disappointed.

'No.' Amy picked up her empty cup and muesli bar wrapper.

'Any orthopaedic cases waiting for referral?' Jennifer asked hopefully.

'Don't think so.' Tom smiled at Jennifer. 'I'm sure there'll be a desperate need to summon Noel Fenton at some stage, however.'

'As long as he's the only one that turns up,' Amy muttered under her breath. She rinsed her cup.

'Don't worry, Amy.' Jennifer had overheard the mutter. She was still smiling at Tom. 'We'll protect you.' She stood up with a reluctant glance at the clock. 'Just don't go apologising to him.'

'No, don't,' Tom Barlow agreed emphatically. 'You've got nothing to apologise for.'

'That's a matter of opinion,' Amy said quietly. 'I think I'll have to disagree.'

'He might forgive you,' Tom warned. 'And then where would you be?'

'Engaged, probably,' Jennifer supplied disgustedly.

'Quite.' Tom settled himself comfortably on the old couch. 'And you wouldn't want that, now, would you?' His innocently questioning gaze didn't falter despite Amy's best withering look. He grinned disarmingly. 'Look, if you're that desperate to marry someone, I'll marry you myself.'

'Great idea!' Jennifer's enthusiasm was instant. She

was making no further effort to leave the staffroom and begin her shift. 'Can I be bridesmaid?'

'Sure.' Tom nodded agreeably.

Amy expelled her breath in an exasperated huff. 'It's you two that should get together,' she said scathingly. 'You're obviously two of a kind.'

Amy stalked away from the staffroom. How could Jennifer treat all this as though it were a big joke? Amy felt let down. Betrayed. Even Janice Healey was more aware of the repercussions than her best friend seemed to be. Amy was on the shelf. Past her 'use by' date. She had thrown away her opportunity to get married and have a family. The fact that Janice gained considerable pleasure from feeling sorry for Amy didn't negate the fact that she understood the magnitude of events. Jennifer never used to lack empathy. Her current attitude probably had to be laid at Tom Barlow's feet.

Amy made for the sorting desk to collect any new patient admissions. Tom Barlow was really quite insufferable. He'd been quite happy to offer his opinions on the relationship of someone he hadn't even been introduced to on Friday night. Now he was quite happy to assume he knew better than Amy what she really wanted. He was just as bad as Nigel Wesley. And Nigel Wesley's mother. What *was* it about her that made her opinions and desires so insignificant?

Amy was assigned a fifty-two-year-old woman who had been sent in by her GP, having presented with chest pain and increasing shortness of breath. Amy helped the woman into a hospital gown and attached electrodes to start monitoring her cardiac rhythm. She attended to the task automatically, her thoughts still elsewhere.

It wasn't as if she was stupid. Certainly not stupid enough to make a choice that everyone else could see was a major mistake. OK, she had to admit to herself that she wasn't madly in love with Nigel Wesley—but where had falling in love got her previously? Badly hurt, that's where. Surely when you weren't blinded by love it was easier to see and accept someone's faults— like a tendency to bad temper, perhaps, and to know whether one could live with them long term.

Amy recorded all the baseline observations for her patient. Pulse and respiration rate, blood pressure, temperature and cardiac rhythm. She could see the ST segment depression on the ECG trace clearly, which indicated that the blood supply to Mrs Johnston's heart muscle was compromised. It could be an easily managed angina attack but it could also be heralding a heart attack.

'The doctor will be in to see you very soon, Mrs Johnston,' Amy reassured the frightened woman. 'And we'll get something to help that chest pain.'

The first resus team call for the day came just after Mrs Johnston's baseline blood samples had been collected and an IV line started. Amy administered the dose of morphine that the consultant, Susan Scott, had ordered. Then she signalled to Janice.

'I've got a resus team call. Keep an eye on Mrs Johnston and call one of the doctors if there's any change.'

'But I've got two patients of my own already,' Janice protested.

'Mrs Johnston needs another set of observation in ten minutes,' Amy said firmly. 'And these blood supplies need to go to the lab straight away.'

The patient was coming through the doors as Amy

joined the team. She caught the last of the ambulance officer's hand-over.

'He apparently staggered onto the road, unaware of where he was. He's got track marks on his arms and pinpoint pupils but denies any IV drug use.'

Amy's brain clicked into gear. 'Full BSI precautions,' she reminded the team. 'Double gloving, aprons and goggles if necessary.' An intravenous drug user was high risk for being HIV positive, and body substance isolation procedures were the team's only protection against the virus.

The team moved quickly as the patient, a young man, was transferred to a bed in Resus 1. Jennifer was the airway nurse on the team again.

'I'm Jennifer,' she told their patient cheerfully as she organised the oxygen supply. 'What's your name?'

'Get stuffed,' the patient responded.

'Can you open your eyes for me?'

The response was even less polite. The patient giggled and repeated his obscenities. Tom smiled at Jennifer, shaking his head briefly. He straightened up from listening to the patient's chest.

'Chest is clear. Breathing's shallow.' He glanced at the high-concentration oxygen mask being used and nodded approval. 'Is he on 15 litres a minute?'

Jennifer nodded.

'What are our baselines, Amy?'

'BP's 110 over 60, respirations 12, heart rate 60, skin cold and clammy.'

Team members had cut away the remainder of the patient's clothing. The registrar was trying to shine a torch in the patient's eyes, which were being held closed.

'What have you taken, mate?'

'Nothing. Bugger off. Ah-h!' The groan turned into a scream that made Amy wince.

'Where's the pain?' Tom queried sharply. The patient's response was incoherent. A rapid head-to-toe assessment by Tom revealed no obvious trauma but the patient was making agonised noises whenever he was touched. 'Let's get baseline bloods away,' Tom ordered the registrar. 'Haemoglobin, white-cell count, packed cell volume and cross-matching.' Tom rattled off the other tests needed. 'I think we'll assume narcotic abuse with those pinpoint pupils. Let's give him 2 mg Narcan. I don't want respirations any more depressed than they are already.'

Amy drew up the opiate antagonist, got Tom to check the syringe and ampoule and then administered the drug into the IV port.

Tom had turned his attention back to the patient's abdomen. His palpation elicited a fresh outburst of loud groans. 'There's guarding and some distension,' Tom reported.

Janice had been checking the pockets of their patient's trousers. 'There's a community services card in here,' she said excitedly. 'The name on it is Sean James. Age twenty-one.'

'Sean?' Jennifer asked. 'Is that your name?' She got no response. Shaking his shoulder a little, she spoke more loudly. 'Sean? Wake up. Open your eyes.'

Amy glanced at the monitors. 'BP's dropped a bit,' she informed Tom. 'Now 100 over 55. Heart rate's up to 80.'

'He's bleeding,' Tom decided. 'There's something going on abdominally, and with the mechanism of injury we've got to suspect a pelvic fracture as well. Are we ready for some X-rays? I want chest, lateral C-spine and pelvis.'

Noel Fenton arrived as soon as the X-rays were ready. 'Was it a lateral compression force?' he asked Tom.

Tom nodded. The car had hit the victim side on.

'What speed was it going?'

'Not that fast. Less than 50 km/h initially and braking hard by the time contact was made.'

'Fast enough to do some major damage,' Noel observed. 'Bucket handle displacement of the hemipelvis and severe disruption to the sacroiliac joint. And look at this...' Noel tapped the viewing screen. 'We've got fractures of both superior and inferior pubic rami on this side. Any urethral damage?'

'Probably. We've gone for a suprapubic rather than a urethral catheter.' Tom puffed out his cheeks thoughtfully. 'We could have some abdominal injuries as well. We're setting up for a peritoneal lavage but I'm not going to send him for laparotomy until we get this fracture stabilised. How soon can we get an external fixator in place?'

'Should only take five to ten minutes,' Noel responded. 'But I can't do one on my own. I'll have to get Nigel Wesley down here.'

'Get on to it,' Tom commanded. 'This chap's going into hypovolaemic shock.'

Stephen's condition had deteriorated considerably since his arrival. The Narcan had reversed the effects of the self administered narcotics but the internal blood loss from the pelvic and abdominal injuries had put him into severe shock, despite the additional IV line Tom had inserted and the speed with which fluid replacement was being done.

Amy checked the nasogastric tube she had just
helped the registrar insert. Stephen James was now un-
conscious and the procedure had not been difficult. As-
pirating the limited stomach contents had also been
easy.

'Set up a peritoneal lavage kit and an external pelvic
fixator,' Tom directed Amy as he returned to the patient's side. 'Let's hope Nigel Wesley doesn't take too
long to get here.'

Amy tried to put aside the dread she felt. Surely this
was the best of circumstances to make contact with
Nigel again. Focused on the patient and with other staff
members present, he could hardly make a scene by
singling her out for personal recriminations or unpleas-
antness. Indeed, when Nigel first arrived he ignored
Amy completely, which was fine by her. It was Tom
who caught the first flak after presenting the case and
showing the X-rays to the consultant.

'What's so urgent about this fixator?' Nigel queried
coldly. 'I'm in the middle of an outpatient clinic.'

'The patient has abdominal rigidity and reduced
bowel sounds. He's already in shock.' Tom's tone was
clipped. 'I'm not about to send him to Theatre for laparotomy until we can stabilise this fracture and get the
bleeding under control.'

'Have you done a peritoneal lavage?'

'We're about to.'

'Well, why don't you get on with that while I have
a better look at these X-rays?' Nigel's tone was deceptively pleasant. He sounded like a parent keeping a grip
on his temper while chastising a badly behaved child.
Tom clearly resented the tone.

'I have a patient who's bleeding out here,' he told
Nigel quietly. 'The most likely cause is retroperitineal

bleeding. I do not want a rupture of haematomata into the peritoneal space, which is likely to lead to uncontrolled and probably fatal haemorrhage. The only way to reduce the rate of this blood loss right now is to stabilise the pelvic ring.' Tom's voice dropped to a level that was almost threatening. 'If you don't want to apply the fixator, then I'll do it myself. It won't be the first time.'

Noel Fenton was standing beside Nigel. His eyes widened fractionally as Nigel glared furiously at Tom. Amy flinched as the gaze flicked towards her.

'I assume you have a Hoffman multifaxial frame available, Nurse?' Nigel snapped.

Amy nodded and swallowed hard. 'We've prepped the iliac crests and I have lignocaine drawn up.'

Nigel turned away to snatch a pair of gloves from the box attached to the wall.

'You'll need to double glove,' Amy told him nervously. 'The patient's HIV status is questionable.'

'Oh, great,' Nigel muttered. Only Amy could hear him. 'My day improves even further.'

Amy sighed. Nigel hated her. He obviously hated Tom Barlow as well. Was that simply due to Tom's siding with and rescue of her at the party, or did Nigel hate everybody today because he'd been humiliated by her? Whatever the reason, working with him was unpleasantly tense. Nigel was critical of her assistance and Amy became increasingly nervous. If she stood close, she was too close. Nigel actually nudged her quite painfully with his elbow. When she held part of the framing connecting the pins which had been inserted over both hips, her hands were precisely in the wrong place for Nigel and Noel to attach the screws. Noel got snapped at as well and he raised a conspira-

torial eyebrow at Amy when the consultant wasn't
looking.

Tom was hovering over the peritoneal lavage kit that
Amy had prepared, but he needed to wait until the orthopaedic consultant was out of the way. He studied
the monitors.

'Let's get another haemoglobin concentration away.
The BP's still dropping a bit,' he commented. 'I'd like
a blood gas, too.'

Amy collected the full test tubes just as Nigel and
Noel completed the application of the pelvic device.
She could swear that Nigel stepped back into her path
deliberately, standing on her foot and causing her stum-
ble and near fall. The result was catastrophic as far as
Amy was concerned. The test tubes flew to the floor
and shattered.

Nigel's expulsion of breath was derogatory. 'Have
you forgotten that this patient is probably HIV positive?' he snarled. 'Are you just trying to see how ef-
fective our BSI precautions might be—or are you physically incapable of doing this job without falling over
occasionally?'

Amy gasped. Apart from Jennifer, nobody in this
department knew about her physical problems. She
would never be able to cope if Nigel said anything
more in front of her colleagues. Amy held her breath,
aware that she was ominously close to bursting into
tears.

Nigel looked down at his blood-spattered shoes.
'You'd better do something about these, hadn't you?'
He shook his head. 'Here we have an already volume-
depleted patient and now you'll have to draw more
blood to replace those samples. Just how much do you
think he can afford to lose?'

Tom spoke calmly. 'We can do without those samples for now.' He nodded at one of the other nurses. 'Cheryl, would you take Mr Wesley down to the sluice room and make up some hypochlorite solution to clean his shoes with?'

'I know where the sluice room is, thank you,' Nigel said acidly. 'I'd prefer to do the job myself. I'm not convinced that any of your staff can perform quite to my standards. *Some* might even be considered a menace.'

Tom ignored him. 'We'll need some for the floor, too, thanks, Cheryl. Amy, I need you to help me with this lavage.'

Nigel stood staring at Tom for several seconds in silence. Tom continued to ignore him and the surgeon turned on his heel and walked out.

Tom didn't appear fazed at all by the disaster with the contaminated blood or the open hostility that Nigel had displayed. 'Jen, let's have a ten per cent head-down tilt. Have you got any lignocaine with adrenaline drawn up, Amy?'

'Yes.' With immense gratitude, Amy turned her attention to the new task. Nigel's expert attempt to put her down enough to destroy her self-confidence could have been successful if it weren't for the ease with which Tom was now handing it back to her. Amy's hands were still shaking slightly as she passed the syringe full of local anaesthetic. Tom's hand closed over hers just long enough to disguise her tremble and allow a smooth passage of the syringe with no mishaps.

Tom gave no direct indication that he considered Nigel's criticism misplaced. He didn't need to. By the time Amy passed him a scalpel, her hands were steady again. When the artery forceps were needed, Amy found she was restored to her normal confident and deft levels of assistance.

Tom noted the positive result of the lavage as more than 10 ml of blood was freely aspirated from the peritoneal cavity. 'He needs an urgent laparotomy. What's the BP doing?'

'Gone up a bit,' Amy reported with satisfaction. 'Ninety-five over seventy.'

'Good. Get on the phone and let Theatre know we're on the way.' Tom smiled. 'Thanks for your assistance, Amy. That was great.'

Amy's flush of pleasure at Tom's praise went a long way towards counteracting the venom Nigel had showered upon her, but its effect was shortlived. Peter Milne was looking for her and he didn't look happy.

'When you get a Resus Team call, Amy, it's vital that you hand over any patients you are currently responsible for to another nurse. If you can't find someone, it's your responsibility to let me know.'

'I did hand over,' Amy said in surprise. 'To Janice.'

'Well, Janice didn't know anything about it,' Peter informed her. 'Neither did any of the other staff. The bloods that should have been sent to the lab are still sitting there and Mrs Johnston was left entirely alone until the alarm alerted us to the fact that she'd gone into ventricular tachycardia.'

'Oh, God,' Amy murmured. 'What happened?'

'Fortunately, it resolved spontaneously. She's been moved to CCU.' Peter looked less disapproving. 'In future, Amy, make sure that you ensure continuity of care for your patients.'

Amy was about to protest her innocence again. If Janice had been too overloaded to supervise Mrs Johnston, she should have known to inform the nurse manager of the situation. Amy could see Janice, standing near the sorting desk, chatting to Laura. As though sensing the observation, Janice looked up and caught Amy's gaze. The smile that accompanied the swish of the sleek bob was less than pleasant and Amy changed her mind about arguing. It was simply her word against Janice's and Peter was right. It had been her responsibility and she should have picked someone more trustworthy than Janice Healey. Amy merely nodded in response to Peter's last admonition.

'Anything you want me to do now, Peter?'

'Take a quick break,' Peter advised. 'That was a tough case you just had.' His expression was cautious. 'I hear Nigel Wesley was a bit hard on you.'

Amy shrugged. 'I guess he has his reasons.'

Peter's smile was understanding. 'So I hear.' He cleared his throat. 'Good for you, anyway, Amy. Are you OK?'

'I'm fine. At least I will be after some coffee.'

Amy eased herself onto the old couch in the staffroom with care. Thanks to her near fall, her leg was now aching abominably. It was almost bad enough to make her consider breaking her long-held rule about not taking any kind of pain relief while on duty. She eyed the sensible black lace-up shoes she wore. Maybe she needed more than the two extra inner soles in the left one. The lift this method gave her shorter leg wasn't quite enough, but there was no way she was going to revert to wearing the orthotic footwear forced on her as an adolescent.

That obviously built-up sole had provided her father with visible evidence of her failure to measure up, but he hadn't been the only one stare at every opportunity.

The shoe had also provided a weapon for other children to dismiss her suitability to belong. Amy had worn the footwear only to keep her mother happy that everything possible was being done to make up for the unfortunate accident. When her mother had died, the motivation had gone.

The padding in Amy's shoe could be concealed. Extra lift if things got difficult could be gained by her habit of walking slightly on tiptoe on her left side. She had become skilled in keeping her balance and had never fallen over at work, but pressure often led to her dismissal of the need to compensate and the result was pain such as she was experiencing now.

Amy touched her thigh. The scarred and misshapen area was also well concealed by keeping her uniform size a shade larger than she needed. It was a matter of pride that no one other than Jennifer knew about her leg. Nigel had come far too close to destroying her confidence in both the personal and professional arena. How could she possibly cope if he made a more successful assault next time? If Tom Barlow wasn't on hand to provide protection and rescue?

Amy's spiralling anxiety was broken when Jennifer bustled into the staffroom.

'You're not going to let Nigel Wesley get away with treating you like that, are you?' Jennifer demanded. 'Make a complaint.'

'What, to go with the one he'll probably be making about me spattering him with contaminated blood? Get real, Jen.'

'And what was Peter on at you about?'

Amy told her friend about the patient being left unattended, thanks to Janice Healey's unhelpfulness. Jennifer was furious.

'You can't just let her get away with it.'

Amy sat further back with a flop, perilously close to tears. 'Everything's a mess,' she said miserably. 'And it's all my fault.' She rubbed her forehead with her hand. 'My father always said I could never do a damned thing right. Maybe it's true.'

'Your father was a bastard,' Jennifer said in her usual succinct style. She put her arm around Amy's shoulders. 'Perhaps that's why you were attracted to Nigel Wesley. They say women look for someone like their father.' She gave Amy a comforting squeeze. 'Well, you don't have to worry about either of them any more.'

'I still have to work with Nigel.'

'Forget him. He's a weasel.' Jennifer grinned at her own wit. 'Nigel Weasely. Don't you love it?'

'I love it,' Amy said obediently.

'And I heard Tom say you were great.' Jennifer paused as she headed back out of the staffroom. 'Hey, now, there's a man who's nothing like your father.'

'Give it a rest, Jen. I'm not interested.'

'You've got something in common, though.'

'What's that?' Amy asked wearily.

'The weasel isn't keen on either of you right now.' Jennifer shook her head in wonder. 'Do you know, I thought they might be actually going to hit each other during that chat about the fixator.'

Jennifer disappeared through the door and Amy pushed herself to her feet to make a cup of coffee. It was true. The antagonism between the two men had been palpable, and it seemed to have been in place long before a difference of professional opinion could have caused it.

What had Tom been doing at the party if the men

had disliked each other on sight? And why would Nigel
take such an instant dislike to Tom? It would be hard
for anyone to dislike Tom. Amy didn't dislike him,
despite the disturbance he had already caused her. She
wasn't interested in him in any romantic sense, of
course, but she certainly couldn't *dislike* him.

Not at all.

CHAPTER FOUR

'NOT funny?' Tom sounded disappointed.

Amy's smile was noticeably half-hearted. She tapped the 'enter' key on the computer and glanced at the patient information form on the desk beside her. The patient's name was Duncan Langley. His age was thirty-six. Amy entered his date of birth into the appropriate slot and then leaned over the sorting-desk counter to where Mr Langley lay on the bed.

'Have you had any hospital admissions in the past two years, Duncan?'

'No. I'm never sick.' Duncan Langley gazed fearfully at the bustle around him.

Amy also took a look around the department. 'Resus 3, thanks,' she instructed the orderly. 'I'll be with you in just a minute, Duncan.'

The chuckle beside Amy reminded her that Tom was persisting in his efforts to make her laugh. He was holding a sheet of paper.

'How 'bout this one?' Tom smiled broadly. '"Impotent" means "distinguished or well known".'

Amy smiled as she typed in Duncan's presenting complaint of chest pain.

'Or "labour pain—getting hurt at work".'

'What's all this?' Laura, the sorting-desk clerk, looked up from her computer screen.

'Tom's got a new dictionary of medical terms,' Amy told her. 'He's going to drive us all mad for the rest of the day.'

'"Cauterise",' Tom announced. '"Made eye contact with her".'

Laura giggled. 'Let me see.' She reached for the paper.

'"Artery",' she read aloud. '"The study of paintings".'

'What about this one?' Tom pointed over Laura's arm. '"Enema—not a friend".'

Janice Healey brushed past Amy. 'What's so funny?' she demanded.

'Ask Tom.' Amy moved away to collect a hospital gown for Duncan from the linen supply. Tom, Laura and Janice were all laughing as she passed the sorting desk a moment later. Amy ignored them. She didn't feel like being amused. Even a week hadn't been long enough to dull the misery the disastrous party had engendered.

'I need to get you into this hospital gown, Duncan,' Amy told her patient. She helped him remove his jacket. 'Then we're going to run a few tests. Tell me again when all this started.'

'I've been feeling sick for a few days,' Duncan said unhappily. 'Nothing much. Just a sore throat and some shivers and sweats. Not enough to keep me from work.'

'And when did the chest pain start?'

'This morning. At work.' Duncan finished unbuttoning his shirt and stripped it off. Amy attached ECG electrodes.

'Did it come on suddenly?'

'Seemed to. Then it kept getting worse. A mate decided I was having a heart attack and brought me in here.'

Amy fastened the string of Duncan's gown and wrapped a BP cuff around his upper arm. 'This will inflate automatically every few minutes,' she told him. 'It might feel a bit tight for a few seconds when it does.' Amy smiled reassuringly. 'I'm just going to take your temperature and then I'll have to go and get a machine that will let me take a more detailed graph of what your heart's doing.' The single trace on the monitor above them wasn't consistent with a heart attack but it didn't look completely normal. Amy went to fetch a twelve-lead ECG machine.

Tom was still standing near the sorting desk. Gareth and Jennifer were now laughing over the list of medical definitions but Jennifer moved quickly away, pushing the suture trolley in Amy's direction.

'We've got a wonderful laceration in cubicle 2,' she told Amy. 'Right down to the bone. I'll get to see what Tom's needlework is like.'

'I'm sure it's fantastic.' Amy removed the box of tissues and other supplies which had been abandoned on top of the ECG machine. She sighed irritably as she noticed the puddle of unidentifiable liquid on the equipment.

'Cheer up,' Jennifer encouraged. 'It'll be lunchtime soon.'

Amy used some tissues to mop up the liquid. 'I think I need a holiday.'

'You had a day off yesterday.'

'I need a long one,' Amy said forlornly. 'Permanent, even.'

'No, you don't,' Jennifer told her crisply. 'You need to snap out of it. Build a bridge, Amy Brooks,' she advised firmly. 'Get over it.'

'What does Amy need to get over?' Tom appeared beside Jennifer.

'What do you think?' Jennifer shook her head wearily.

Tom's smile was understanding. 'Enough to make even an angel's wings droop for a while. We'll have to find something to cheer her up, won't we, Jen?' Tom grinned at Jennifer. 'Can't have a sad angel in Emergency, can we? It's not a good look.'

Jennifer laughed. 'Come on, Tom. We've got a leg to put back together.'

Amy wheeled the ECG machine back to Resus 3. Jennifer sounded fed up with her and Amy wasn't surprised. She was fed up with herself. She clipped on the chest electrodes and attached the ankle- and wristbands that would analyse the electrical activity of Duncan's heart from all directions. This was a clear-cut task with an achievable short-term goal. Amy could cope easily with that. But how could she get past the emptiness that the sudden removal of her long-term goals had created? It wasn't just the wrench of a setback along the way. It was more that the goalposts had vanished. There was nothing to aim for. How could she build a bridge and get over it when she had no idea what direction she should even aim towards?

Gareth came to check Duncan as Amy finished the twelve-lead trace. The consultant gave the patient a thorough check. Finally he removed the earpieces of his stethoscope.

'Clear pericardial rub,' he commented to Amy before smiling at their patient. 'You've got pericarditis, Duncan, which can be a complication of a viral illness and should clear up completely within a couple of days. It's very rarely associated with any major complications but we'll keep a close eye on you for a day or two.' The consultant turned back to Amy. 'Give

Cardiology a call. I'll have a chat to the registrar when she comes down.'

'What's going to happen now?' Duncan asked Amy.

'I expect you'll be admitted to the CCU. That's the coronary care unit. At least initially,' Amy told him. 'They'll keep a monitor on, like this one, and they'll give you some anti-inflammatory treatment and something more for the pain if you need it.'

'It does hurt.' Duncan's face twisted. 'And I feel miserable.'

'I know.' Amy was sympathetic. 'But it's not a heart attack, Duncan, and it'll get better quickly. You're going to be fine.'

The staffroom was empty when Amy entered a few minutes later. She ate her sandwiches with little enjoyment. She wished her own misery had a physical cause that would clear up as fast as Duncan Langley's. Was she ever going to feel fine again? Jennifer was right. She *had* to snap out of it. She had to find herself a new direction that wasn't dependent on someone else. Specifically, a male someone.

She didn't have to look far afield to find some role models. There was the consultant, Susan Scott, and one of the nurse managers, Angela Parkinson. Angela wasn't much older than Amy. Neither woman was married or had children. They were both successful and engrossed in their careers. To outward appearances they seemed like very settled and happy people. Amy could do a lot worse than aspire to be like them.

The pace in the department picked up in the early afternoon. The cubicles were full. Two registrars were busy examining the patients they contained. Tom, Jennifer and several other staff were dealing with a nasty compound fracture of the lower leg in Resus 2.

It was Amy who received the next patient brought in from the ambulance bay. The middle-aged woman looked extremely unwell.

'This is Jean Cranford. She's fifty-one years old with a past history of MI and hypertension.'

Amy glanced at the GP's covering letter as she listened to the ambulance officer. Mrs Cranford had come in from a rural area and it had been nearly two hours since the doctor had seen her.

'She's been unwell for two days with a cough and extreme lethargy. Her neighbour found her this morning, very confused and short of breath, and the doctor was called.'

Amy took hold of the woman's hand. 'Hello, Mrs Cranford.'

Her patient looked around vaguely before trying to focus on Amy's face.

'Do you know where you are at the moment?' Amy queried gently.

Jean Cranford closed her eyes as she shook her head. Then she began coughing, struggling to sit further upright. She pushed the oxygen mask away from her face. Amy grabbed a facecloth from a nearby linen trolley as pink-tinged froth appeared at the corners of Mrs Cranford's mouth.

'You're in hospital, Mrs Cranford.' Amy wiped her patient's mouth and replaced the oxygen mask. She didn't like the blue tinge to the woman's face at all. 'My name's Amy and we're going to take good care of you.' Amy looked behind her at the drawn curtains. Jean Cranford was seriously unwell with what appeared to be heart failure. They needed a resus area but they all looked occupied.

Tom emerged from behind the curtain to Resus 2.

He took in the scene rapidly. 'Resus 3 is available,' he said calmly. 'It's just minus a bed.'

'I'll get one.' An ambulance officer moved away quickly.

Tom was eyeing the paperwork in Amy's hand. 'What is Mrs Cranford's blood pressure like?'

'Last reading was 140 over 100. Heart rate of 105.'

'The oxygen saturation was eighty five per cent until we started oxygen,' the second ambulance officer told Tom. 'Then it came up to ninety. The GP put an IV line in but it tissued about an hour ago.'

Tom was lifting the blanket covering Mrs Cranford's legs. Amy could see the obvious swelling of her feet and ankles. She helped move the stretcher towards Resus 3 as the empty hospital bed was maneuvered into position.

'We'll need a chest X-ray and ECG,' Tom told Amy. 'I'll want arterial blood gases, baseline bloods and an urgent echocardiogram.'

Amy nodded. She was helping to position their patient. 'Let's get you sitting up a bit more, Mrs Cranford.' Amy pulled the bed end up to a ninety degree angle. 'It will help your breathing a bit.' Jean Cranford was struggling to breathe now and looking very distressed.

'Give her some GTN, stat.' Tom was fitting his stethoscope to his ears. 'And let's get a new IV line in.'

More staff appeared and a registrar was given the task of gaining arterial access for blood-gas measurement. Janice applied ECG electrodes and a BP cuff. Amy was ripping packages open and handing equipment to Tom, who seemed to use it as fast as she could keep up the supply. The angiocath was in place and

bloods had been drawn by the time she hooked up a
bag of IV fluids and attached the giving set. Amy only
just reached for the connecting plug to hand it to Tom
before he had to request it.

'Draw up 5 mg morphine for slow IV administration
over three to five minutes,' Tom ordered. 'We'll need
to keep a close eye on the respiration rate.'

The morphine eased Mrs Cranford's distress but the
effectiveness of her breathing didn't improve. Tom was
frowning at the ECG screen. 'What's going on here?'
he murmured.

Amy looked at the odd trace and immediately
checked the electrode placement. She unclipped two
electrodes and swapped their positions. Janice looked
up from writing the patient details on the blood test
tubes.

'Oops, sorry.' Janice flashed Tom an apologetic
glance.

Tom seemed unperturbed. He was still watching the
monitor. 'That looks a bit better. No sign of an acute
MI at this stage.' He turned to Amy. 'I'm not happy
with the oxygen saturation level. Draw up 40 mg of
frusemide, would you, please, Amy?'

'I have already.' Amy had anticipated the need for
a diuretic to combat the fluid build-up in Mrs
Cranford's lungs. She handed Tom the syringe with the
empty ampoule of the drug it contained taped to the
barrel. Tom merely nodded, his attention now turned
to the registrar. 'Let's get a urethral catheter in.' He
picked up his stethoscope again. 'Mrs Cranford? How's
the breathing feel at the moment?' He leaned closer to
their patient. 'Mrs Cranford?'

The woman's eyes opened but then fluttered shut
again. Tom listened to her chest in silence.

'BP's dropped,' Amy warned him. 'One hundred over seventy-five. Respirations down to twelve.'

'Her level of consciousness is dropping, too.' Tom looked at Janice. 'Use a bag mask to assist ventilation for the moment. Amy, we might need to intubate and ventilate. Can you set up?'

The cardiology registrar arrived as Amy set up the equipment Tom had requested. After consultation, the doctors started a dobutamine infusion. Results from the various blood tests began to come back and the echo-cardiology technician arrived, pushing her machine. Amy noted the increased urine output in the catheter bag with satisfaction after the echo had been completed. As the fluid build-up the heart failure had caused began to recede, Mrs Cranford's breathing improved and the level of oxygen in her bloodstream rose. When their patient's condition had stabilised enough to move her to the CCU, Amy emerged from Resus 3 to find that patient numbers in the department were still high. She found herself with three new cubicles to monitor.

Young Charlene Curruthers had given school a miss, gone to a local video-games parlour and had suffered an epileptic seizure, precipitated by the bright, flashing lights. Severely confused after the seizure, Charlene had now recovered and wasn't being co-operative. She was refusing to supply the name of her next of kin or give her address.

'You can't tell my mum. I'll get into trouble for skipping school.'

'You're going to need treatment, Charlene,' Amy explained. 'They need to find out why you had a seizure and maybe give you some medication to make sure it doesn't happen again.'

'Nothing happened,' Charlene said stubbornly.

'I know you don't remember what happened,' Amy said. 'But lots of people saw you, and your friend Annabelle was with you at the time.' Amy smiled at the silent and terrified teenager glued to the seat beside the bed.

'It's true, Charlene. You'd better tell them.'

'No. And don't you tell either or you won't be my friend any more.'

'The fact that you don't even remember being brought to hospital in the ambulance shows that it took a while for the electrical activity in your brain to settle down,' Amy continued patiently. 'Do you remember what the doctor told you about epilepsy?'

Charlene shook her head and looked mutinous. Amy decided it was time to get firmer. She could hear her young patient in the next cubicle crying miserably. 'Look, Charlene. You're under age and we can't treat you until we contact your parents. We'll find the information out anyway. It'll just take longer.'

Charlene pressed her lips together grimly. Amy sighed. 'OK. If that's the way you want it.' She eyed Annabelle's uniform. 'Girls' High, isn't it? Right. I'll just ring your headmistress and see what she can tell us.'

'No!' Charlene's bottom lip quivered.

'We have to talk to someone, Charlene,' Amy said more gently. 'Would you rather it was your mum?'

'No.' Charlene chewed the inside of her cheek. 'I guess you could call my dad,' she offered reluctantly.

'Good girl,' Amy said when she'd written the details down. 'I'll get Laura to call him and I'll be back to see you soon.'

Amy delivered the slip of paper to Laura and then hurried back to cubicle 1. The baby was still crying.

'Has he vomited again?'

'Yes, and I can't get him to settle. He's refusing to feed.' The mother looked weary and Amy looked more closely at three-month-old William. His fontanelle wasn't depressed and his skin colour wasn't mottled or clammy, which would have indicated severe dehydration, but the baby was running a high fever and his eyes looked a little sunken. He had vomited several times since he'd come in twenty minutes previously and if he continued to refuse breast-feeding he was going to need IV fluid replacement. Severe dehydration was dangerous in infants and Amy was worried about William.

'I'll get the doctor to come and see you as soon as possible,' Amy told William's mother. 'I'm sorry things are so busy.'

Amy's third patient was a young woman who was also running a fever but her main complaint was severe abdominal pain. Blood tests had been taken and an ultrasound examination was ordered, and Amy helped her patient to the toilet to collect a urine sample for a pregnancy test while the registrar was checking baby William. She then returned to cubicle 2 to assist the registrar to insert an IV line in William's scalp vein and start an infusion of fluid.

Charlene's father arrived as William was taken to the paediatric observation unit and the registrar went to examine the woman with abdominal pain. Charlene was referred for a neurology consult but the registrar was unable to see her for more than an hour so Amy took Charlene through to a bed in the EOA. The adjacent bed held a patient who had obviously needed a

surgical referral. The case must have been unusual
enough to require the presence of a consultant as well
as a registrar, because Murray Brownlie emerged as the
curtain was pulled back.

Amy smiled at the surgeon, trying to catch his eye.
She'd love to ask how Daniel Lever had progressed
over the last week. Maybe he'd even been discharged
by now. Murray Brownlie saw Amy. He apparently
saw right through Amy. She was invisible. The eager
query died and Amy watched the surgeon and his registrar walk away. So much for being impressed by
Amy's knowledge and interest in her job. And so much
for visiting the wards or observing in Theatre.

Any special status that her association with Nigel
had conferred had clearly been summarily withdrawn.
It was hardly unexpected. What was unexpected was
how painful the withdrawal was. Amy had had no inkling of how much she might miss the honorary status
and the attention and opportunities it had created.

Amy's patient with the abdominal pain was diagnosed with an acute kidney infection that required admission and antibiotic therapy. Having dealt with her
transfer to the ward, Amy wasn't surprised to find that
well over an hour had passed since she'd last really
drawn breath. She hadn't even seen Tom since they'd
worked together to stabilise Mrs Cranford's episode of
heart failure. She had to smile when she saw he was
still clutching a now rather dog-eared sheet of paper.

'"Outpatient",' he greeted Amy. '"A patient who
has fainted".'

Jennifer came out of Resus 2 with an armload of
dirty linen. She pushed it into the red bag designated
for material contaminated with blood and other body

fluids. She grinned at Tom. 'I like nitrates being cheaper than day rates.'

'My favourite is rectum,' Tom decided.

Jennifer nodded in agreement. 'It's brilliant.'

Amy had to ask. 'And what *does* rectum mean?'

Tom kept a straight face. 'Darn near killed him,' he said solemnly.

Amy laughed, a delighted chortle of mirth that took her unawares.

'Finally!' Tom was now grinning broadly. 'I knew you could do it, angel.'

The curtain to Resus 2 opened again and Noel joined them. 'Hey, Tom,' he said. 'Are you going to come ice skating with me and Jen tonight? There's a few of us going.'

'Sounds great,' Tom nodded. 'You coming, Amy?'

'No. I can't skate.' Amy avoided looking at Tom. She tried to sound nonchalant but the effect of the nickname Tom had bestowed on her was difficult to analyse. She shouldn't like it. She should probably discourage it, but something was stopping her.

'Neither can I,' Tom told her. 'Learning something new is half the fun, and a bit of exercise never hurts.'

'You'd know,' Amy agreed. 'You've been here for a week and from what I've heard you've already joined the mountain bike club, found two squash partners, been enlisted for a tennis tournament and you've put your name down for the Christmas tramping trip to Milford.' She eyed Tom curiously. 'Is there any form of exercise you don't do?'

'Ice skating,' Tom responded promptly. 'But I plan to rectify that tonight. You should come, too.'

Jennifer and Amy exchanged a meaningful glance in the silence that fell. Tom raised an eyebrow thoughtfully before smoothly transferring his attention to Noel. 'Have a look at these, Noel,' he invited, handing over the sheet. 'It's provided a bit of entertainment around here today. It even made Amy laugh.'

Amy moved away. A BP cuff had fallen from its stand and the curly cord was threatening to snag on the next wheel that went past. As she straightened to re-fasten the cuff, she was disconcerted to find Tom beside her again. The surprise factor caused an odd tingle that went right through her body.

'I just wanted to thank you for your assistance with Mrs Cranford.' Tom was smiling warmly. 'You were great.'

Amy shrugged modestly. She was still trying to shake off the tingling sensation.

'I mean it,' Tom insisted. 'Not only did you do your job brilliantly but you saved me trying to diagnose a very strange ECG by noticing when someone else wasn't doing their job quite as well.'

'We're a team,' Amy said lightly. 'Next time it'll probably be me that makes a mistake.'

'I doubt that. Listen, if ice skating really isn't your scene, why don't we find something a little less stren-uous to do tonight?'

Amy found herself looking into those brown eyes just a little too long. The sensation of being touched, the memory of that kiss, was always there. Expe-riencing it repeatedly had a kind of addictive effect. It was a bit like sticking your finger through a candle flame, wondering how slowly you could do it without burning yourself. She was aware of the curtain to Resus 2 moving again, but it wasn't until the figure ap-proached them that she realised it was Nigel. He was staring at them very blatantly and Amy felt the clutch of a now familiar, and far less addictive, tension. Tom stiffened. Amy could almost see his hackles rise.

'You've managed to find time to assess young Gerald's fracture. That's great.' Tom's smile was stilted. 'What's the verdict, then, Nigel?'

'We'll be taking him up to Theatre shortly.' Nigel's tone was clipped. He was using as much effort as Tom to sound polite. Amy risked a nervous glance. 'There's one or two things I'd like to discuss first, if you have a moment.' Nigel's tone suggested that it was unlikely Tom would be required elsewhere.

'Of course.' Tom's obliging reply was a little over-done.

Amy moved away, ill at ease, but not before Nigel had returned her glance. Expecting to encounter the backlash of the simmering hostility between the two men, Amy was pleasantly surprised when Nigel merely gave her a cool nod before continuing his conversation with Tom.

An orderly was talking to Laura. 'Where's the woman being admitted to Ward 23?'

'That's my patient,' Amy told him. 'She's in cubicle 6. I'll give you a hand. I need to check that her observations are up to date.'

Amy went as far as the main corridor before saying goodbye to her patient. Returning to Emergency, she was dismayed to find herself alone in the corridor with Nigel.

'How are you, Amy?'

'Fine.' Amy glanced up only briefly. 'Pretty busy, as usual.'

'It's a busy department,' Nigel concurred. 'And not just in working hours.'

Amy wasn't sure how to respond. Nigel's tone

wasn't hostile but some sort of criticism was implied. Was it directed at her?

'Ice skating isn't my scene either.' Nigel broke the short but awkward silence. 'As you know.' He was smiling now. Amy could hear it and she knew exactly what the smile would be like without looking. It would convey understanding and an acceptance of her lack of ability in physical pursuits. Nigel's aversion to anything too strenuous came from a lack of desire rather than ability, but it had given them common ground. Part of the base they had built their relationship on.

Nigel paused again. He cleared his throat uncomfortably and waited as a nurse escorted a small group of people past them.

'I must apologise for my reference to your lack of balance the other day.'

Amy remained silent as she remembered the incident of dropping the blood samples. Had her impression that Nigel had deliberately stepped into her path been wrong?

'I was angry,' Nigel admitted. 'My temper gets the better of me sometimes.' He made a self-deprecating sound. 'One of my many faults, I know.'

Amy met his gaze. If Nigel knew his faults and was prepared to apologise for them, did that make them excusable? She had plenty of faults of her own.

'I owe you an apology, too,' Amy said quietly. 'To tell you the truth, Nigel, I've spent the last week feeling more than a little ashamed of myself.'

Nigel nodded, as though that was only to be expected. He even smiled tolerantly. 'Why don't we have a bit of a chat about things?' he suggested.

Amy hesitated. 'I didn't really think you'd want to speak to me again.' A private chat with Nigel concerning their former relationship wasn't something she had prepared herself for.

'Alcohol can be blamed for quite a few misunderstandings,' Nigel murmured. 'I think we've both had time to consider events a little more clearly, don't you?'

Amy nodded slowly. Was Nigel offering her a way out of this mess? A chance to put things back the way they were? She nodded more firmly. Another nurse hurried past them. Nigel cleared his throat again, more purposefully this time.

'What about meeting for dinner?' He frowned at an approaching bed. 'That way we could talk without constant interruptions.'

As if on cue, Nigel's beeper sounded.

'Excuse us.' The orderly wanted more room for the bed.

'OK,' Amy said hurriedly. 'Yes, I think I'd like that, Nigel.'

'Good.' Nigel nodded briskly. 'I'll contact you as soon as I've made a reservation.'

Amy smiled at Jennifer with some bemusement as she returned to the emergency department. 'Guess what?'

'You're going to come ice skating with us?' Jennifer looked hopeful. 'I'm sure you could manage.'

'I'm going out to dinner. With Nigel.'

'What?' Jennifer's face emptied of expression. *'Why?'*

'Because he asked me,' Amy said carefully. 'And because I'd like the chance to put things right.'

'Put what right?' Tom dropped a set of patient case notes on the desk.

Amy groaned inwardly. Tom had a knack of appearing at just the wrong moment and he clearly had no compunction about muscling in on other people's business. It was time he knew his interest wasn't welcome.

'This is a private conversation,' Amy informed him coolly.

'Amy's going to dinner with the weasel,' Jennifer told Tom helpfully. 'I suspect she's going to grovel.'

Amy glared at Jennifer despairingly. Tom frowned at Amy.

'You can't be serious.'

'For God's sake,' Amy snapped. 'Nigel isn't some sort of monster. He's actually a very nice person when you get to know him.'

Tom's raised eyebrow was eloquent. Amy transferred her glare. 'You don't even know anything about him,' she accused Tom.

'Don't I?'

'Not much,' Amy said dismissively. 'Maybe you haven't got off to the best start but first impressions can be misleading, you know. Sometimes what's on the surface isn't the most important thing.'

Tom's expression became watchful. 'I couldn't agree more, Amy,' he said softly. 'I hope you'll bear that in mind.'

Amy waited until Tom had moved out of earshot before turning to Jennifer. 'What was that supposed to mean?'

Jennifer shrugged. 'Maybe Tom thinks he knows more about Nigel than you think he does.'

'Ha!' Amy wasn't quite sure she followed Jennifer's logic but she didn't have time to try and decipher the odd exchange. She had more patients waiting.

Why were so many people throwing up today? Amy

had an armful of unpleasantly soiled linen when she passed the sorting desk a short time later. Laura waved a scrap of paper at her.

'Message for you, Amy.'

Amy grimaced at her full load. 'I'll get it in a minute. I've got to get rid of this lot.'

It was Tom in the corridor this time when Amy emerged from the sluice room.

'Laura asked me to give you this.' He handed over the folded scrap of paper and turned away abruptly.

Amy looked at the message. It had the name of a nearby pub popular with hospital staff and the time of 7 p.m. She frowned in puzzlement. Nigel usually chose upmarket and quiet restaurants. Amy found herself smiling seconds later. Nigel was making an effort here. It would be far less tense for them to talk in a relaxed and casual atmosphere. Maybe he also realised that she preferred the simple type of meal the bar could produce, like a plate of nachos or a bowl of spicy wedges. If Nigel was prepared to forgo his own preferences for her then maybe they had a real chance of discussing the other issues their relationship faced. Like his mother. Like his assumption that he could move her to another country without bothering to seek her approval first.

If Nigel could make an effort then so could Amy. She dressed carefully for the date. Casual but smart in dressy jeans, a silk shirt and a soft jacket in her favourite colour of coppery brown. The pub wasn't too crowded when she arrived just before 7 p.m. Amy ordered a drink which she carried to an empty corner table. Orange juice. She wasn't going to risk any kind of alcohol intake this evening. By 7.20 Amy was starting her second glass of juice. Perhaps Nigel had been held up in Theatre. By 7.40 she'd changed her mind. Nigel had decided not to come. Had he, in fact, set this up in order to punish her?

The new influx of patrons deepened Amy's humiliation. The crowd of emergency department staff included both Jennifer and Tom. Trying to look as though she sat in pubs by herself all the time, Amy was nonchalantly reading the blackboard menu when she knew she'd been spotted.

'Amy! What on earth are you doing here? I thought you were going out to dinner?'

'I am.'

'What, here?' Jennifer looked astonished. 'I thought you were meeting Nigel.'

'I am,' Amy repeated.

'You said 7 p.m. You rushed out while I was still in the shower.'

Amy wished that Tom would disappear. It was just typical of him to be avidly listening in on someone else's conversation.

'So he's a bit late,' she said defensively. 'I'm not bothered.'

Jennifer sat down at her table. 'It's nearly 8 o'clock, Amy. He's not coming.'

Tom leaned on the back of the remaining chair. 'Come out with us, angel,' he said kindly. 'We're just having a drink before we hit the skating rink. You can't stay here all by myself.'

The nickname conveyed a familiarity that wasn't welcome right now. 'I can if I want to,' Amy muttered rebelliously. 'Nigel's coming. He said he would and he's never let me down before.'

Jennifer and Tom exchanged a glance. 'Let's have a drink,' Jennifer suggested. 'I'll get them.'

'Great. I'll have a beer, thanks,' Tom responded. 'Amy?'

'Nothing for me, thanks.' Amy watched Jennifer head to the bar with dismay. She was left alone with Tom who now moved to sit down on the chair. The other staff members were still ordering their drinks. Janice was accepting a glass of wine from Peter.

'Don't waste your life, Amy,' Tom said quietly. 'Waiting for Nigel Wesley.'

Amy was silent. The last hour *had* been miserably empty.

'It's very easy to pick things up and play with them when they're lying around,' Tom continued casually. 'It's just as easy to put them down again. If it's more of an effort to catch hold of them, then you know it's something you want to catch.' Tom paused. 'And keep hold of,' he added.

'You're full of advice, aren't you?' Amy couldn't quite manage the waspish tone she would have preferred.

'Ah, yes, little grasshopper,' Tom agreed lightly. He grinned at Amy. 'And my advice is this. Get a life and good things will happen for you.'

'I've got a life, thanks.'

'Make it better. Come out with me.'

'On a *date*?' Amy was horrified. 'No way!'

Tom smiled mischievously. 'I've never been let down so gently. No, not a date, angel. Come out with a group of friends and enjoy yourself. You don't have to skate. Peter's wife is just coming to watch. She's way too pregnant to skate.'

Amy eyed the laughing group still gathered near the bar. Jennifer was coming back towards them, carrying three drinks. Janice was trailing after her. The extra glass of wine was clearly intended for Amy and she smiled as she accepted the offering. Friends were important. Friends were all she had at the moment.

'Tom's persuaded me to break out of here,' Amy told Jennifer.

'Fantastic.'

Janice's blue eyes widened as she reached the table. 'You're going out? With *Tom*?'

'It's not a date.' Tom gave Amy a reassuring glance. 'Amy's coming ice skating with all of us.'

Janice looked relieved. She leaned forward to smile at Tom and touch her glass to his. 'Cheers, Tom.'

Amy caught Jennifer's wink but couldn't share her friend's resigned amusement. She sipped her own drink. Cheers, indeed. Why should she care if Janice was turning on the charm for Tom's benefit? It wasn't as if she was going on a date with the man. She was just going out to enjoy the company of a group of friends.

And Tom Barlow just happened to be one of them.

CHAPTER FIVE

THE small boy in cubicle 2 wasn't arousing any sympathy in Nurse Amy Brooks.

'If you try and bite me again, Troy, I'm going to get cross,' she warned.

Troy's mother glared at Amy. 'It's not his fault,' she said belligerently.

Amy kept her agreement to herself. The woman's son had clearly been disadvantaged in both the nature and nurture stakes. Troy poked his tongue out at Amy. She resisted the urge to reciprocate.

'We're just waiting for the doctor from the ENT department to come and see Troy,' Amy said as pleasantly as she could manage.

'Why can't *you* do something?' Troy's mother demanded irritably. 'It's only a bit of plastic, for God's sake.'

'Yes,' Amy agreed. 'But Troy has pushed it so far up his nose that it may have done some damage. There's also the possibility that he might inhale it if it's not removed carefully. That could be difficult because he's not terribly co-operative, is he?'

He wasn't the only one. Troy's mother looked mutinous. 'I'm not sitting around here all day. I need a smoke.'

Troy aimed a kick at his mother's shins. She retaliated with a swipe that her son dodged with practised ease. The four-year-old eyed Amy's legs.

'I'll be back in a few minutes,' Amy excused herself

hurriedly. 'Please, don't let Troy wander anywhere.' She took a despairing glance at the packet of cigarettes the woman was fishing from her handbag. 'And you definitely can't smoke in here.'

Amy was gritting her teeth as she helped herself to a cup of water from the cooler. Personality and behaviour aside, she had to concede that it probably wasn't entirely Troy's fault. She wasn't *going* to get cross. She'd been cross ever since she'd got out of bed after a largely sleepless night. The lack of rest, in turn, had been due to the fact that her bad mood had started well before she'd even gone to bed.

It wasn't the fact that she hadn't been able to participate in the ice skating that had upset her. It wasn't even that she'd had to sit and watch Janice hanging onto Tom for balance and thoroughly enjoying her own lack of ability. It certainly hadn't been caused by anything as trivial as witnessing Tom examining Janice's ankle after she'd fallen over, even though everybody there had seen that her agony had been somewhat overdone.

'Don't scowl, Amy,' Laura advised. 'It gives you wrinkles.'

'I need to scowl,' Amy growled. 'I'm in a really bad mood.'

'He's a horrible child,' Laura sympathised. 'Puts you off ever becoming a parent, doesn't it?'

Amy grimaced. 'It certainly doesn't help.' Thinking about her chances of ever becoming a parent wasn't likely to help much either.

Jennifer emerged from cubicle 5 with a small tray. She was heading for the sharps disposal bin when Laura caught her eye.

'Amy's not happy.'

'No.' Jennifer watched Amy crumple her paper cup and throw it in the rubbish bin. 'And if Nigel Wesley shows his face in here today, you'd better keep all sharp objects away from her.' Jennifer grinned. 'On second thoughts, line up a whole tray of them.'

'I thought it was all on again after that dinner last night.'

'Dinner?' Jennifer echoed. 'What dinner? He had no intention of showing up. The creep,' she added with relish.

Laura looked outraged. 'He used me to help set it up,' she said. 'I took the message. I'm really sorry, Amy.'

Amy shrugged. 'Not your fault, Laura.'

'He really is a weasel, isn't he?' Laura looked at Jennifer who nodded vigorously.

'You said it.'

Amy didn't bother to try and defend Nigel. If it had been a set-up then it was the last straw. Amy was more than cross. She was angry. If his non-appearance had been genuinely unavoidable then she deserved an explanation and an apology. After six hours on duty today already, an apology was clearly not a matter of any urgency. Amy's mood simmered on till the end of her shift. She actually took some pleasure in subduing Troy firmly enough for the ENT registrar to remove the foreign object from his nasal passage. She was also pleased that it had taken a long time for the registrar to turn up. It was just as well Tom wasn't on duty. Amy had never felt less angelic in her life.

It proved more difficult to maintain the rage the following day. Was it just because Tom was back on duty that the whole department had a more cheerful atmosphere? Janice wasn't bothering to limp much any more and Nigel's firm wasn't on call so there was no danger of having to face a confrontation even when the traffic accident victims that came in mid-afternoon had multiple injuries that were largely orthopaedic.

Several people with minor problems arrived first but the resus team was kept in reserve for the more seriously injured victims who had been trapped in their car for some time. They turned out to be a young couple, Cathy and Jack Hanson, whose car had been involved in a head-on collision and then rear-ended by a third vehicle.

Jack was the most critically injured of all the people coming in from the scene. He had major chest and abdominal injuries and the resus team was struggling to keep him alive. He arrested twice before they were able to intubate and ventilate him. Despite aggressive efforts to replace the blood he was losing, his pressures continued to drop and it was Tom who suggested the immediate thoracotomy to allow cross-clamping of the aorta. This desperate procedure could help restore perfusion pressure to the brain and coronary arteries while intra-abdominal haemorrhage was controlled.

There was a moment's stunned silence amongst the resus team. Surgically opening someone's chest was a procedure very rarely attempted in this emergency department, but Tom had had considerable experience in Chicago. Amy rapidly located the seldom-used trolley. This was Jack Hanson's only chance. He couldn't wait long enough to get to Theatre.

A consultant surgeon was called urgently and was on his way to assist, but the team was ready long before he arrived. Amy had worked as a theatre nurse for several years before she'd started in Emergency. She wasn't fazed by the dramatic turn of events, quickly scrubbing up and donning gloves and gown to assist the doctors. The patient was already anaesthetised and ventilated. Jennifer was responsible for prepping his chest and spreading sterile drapes wherever possible.

Janice went as white as a sheet as the small circular saw was used to cut through Jack's sternum and she was taken away by another staff member before she fainted. Even Jennifer looked pale as Tom deployed the rib-spreaders to open up the chest further, resulting in an astonishing spillage of accumulated blood. There was no hope of controlling the bleeding in the field by suction. The trauma had ruptured Jack's diaphragm and the bleeding from abdominal injuries was freely entering his chest.

'Clamp, thanks, Amy.' Tom was struggling to even locate the major blood vessel he wanted to control.

'And another one.'

'Pressure's dropping,' someone warned.

'Gone into V. tachy,' someone else warned.

The dangerous cardiac rhythm progressed into ventricular fibrillation and Jack Hanson suffered another cardiac arrest. Tom reached into his chest and applied cardiac massage by hand while the small internal defibrillator paddles were charged up. His face was tense as he watched the monitor.

'No change,' he stated. 'Charge again—30 joules.' His hand was cradling the heart again, squeezing rhythmically as he spoke.

The surgeon arrived and had difficulty getting close to the patient. It seemed like half the department's staff were crammed into the area, watching and hoping for a successful result. The hope was short-lived. The doctors present quickly agreed that nothing more could be done. Tom looked grim.

'You gave it your best shot,' the surgeon told him quietly. 'Thoracotomy for blunt-chest injury and cardiac arrest is very rarely successful.'

'It was the abdominal bleeding I was hoping to control,' Tom responded. 'I've seen it work. We were just too late. He'd pretty well bled out by the time we got anywhere near the aorta.'

Amy looked at the pools of blood on the floor, the soaked drapes and the open chest of their patient. She'd never seen so much spilt blood in her life. Jack Hanson hadn't stood a chance. Curious staff members were dispersing as the nurse manager on duty, Angela, delegated cleaning-up duties. Amy waited for instructions. She watched Tom closely, concerned at how weary he looked as he finished his conversation with the surgeon.

His gaze finally met Amy's. For once the eye contact seemed to beg a response rather than reach out to touch her.

'I'm sorry it wasn't successful, Tom.' Amy smiled tentatively. 'It was a brave thing to try.' She looked away from him, suddenly discomfited by the length of time their gaze had held. 'Are you going to close the chest again?'

'His wife was brought in as well, wasn't she?'

Amy nodded sadly. 'She arrived a few minutes after Jack. I heard her calling out for him.'

'She may want to see him,' Tom said slowly. 'We'll close up enough for this to be hidden by drapes.'

'Do you need my help?'

'No, thanks, Amy. I'll manage.' Tom watched Jennifer begin the task of removing the life-support tubing. 'It'll take a few minutes to get tidied up in here. Why don't you go and see his wife? I'll be with you as soon as I can. If she isn't already aware of what's been going on, we'll break the news together.'

Jack's wife Cathy was in Resus 6, as far away from the resuscitation attempt on her husband as had been possible. Due to the number of staff involved and the excited conversations that must have been ongoing, Amy knew it was quite likely that Cathy had been aware of the critical situation. Even so, it would take the formal breaking of the news from an official source before any last desperate hopes would have to give way to reality.

The registrar with Cathy saw Amy before she got near the bed. He raised his eyebrows and his face fell at Amy's almost imperceptible head shake. Motioning Amy to one side of the room, the registrar spoke quietly.

'Cathy's thirty-two weeks pregnant. She's been seen by the O and G team and had an ultrasound done. The baby appears to be fine.'

Amy nodded.

'Cathy's got a whiplash injury and a nasty fracture/dislocation of her left elbow. Orthopaedics is coming but they're still a bit tied up with one of the other accident victims. We've had seven people in from this. I'm just going to chase up results on someone else.'

'Who's Cathy's nurse?'

'Janice was in here earlier.' The registrar sighed. 'She was limping around looking washed out and like she might burst into tears at any moment. I sent her off to sit down and I was going to find someone who might be of more support for Cathy.' He looked at Amy hopefully. 'Can you stay with her?'

'I was going to, anyway,' Amy confirmed. 'Tom's coming in to talk to her about Jack.'

Amy moved to the head of the bed and took hold of the patient's hand. 'Hi, Cathy,' she said softly. 'My name's Amy. I'm one of the nurses on the team that has been looking after Jack.'

Cathy's neck was in a brace. Sticky tape across her forehead and onto the backboard prevented any movement of her head, but her eyes swivelled with frantic appeal.

'Is he all right?' Cathy was searching for the answer in Amy's expression. 'Oh, God. *No!*' she whispered brokenly.

'I'm so sorry, Cathy,' Amy said gently. 'We did everything we could. He was just too badly injured. The doctor who was in charge is coming to talk to you in a minute. He'll be able to answer questions for you better than I can.'

Cathy was sobbing. She tried to gain control. 'We'd just been out shopping.' Cathy sounded disbelieving. 'To choose a pram. Jack was so excited about this baby.'

'I'm sorry,' Amy repeated. She held onto Cathy's hand.

'What's going to happen?' Cathy cried. 'Can I see him? Please, I have to see him.'

'Soon,' Amy promised. 'I need to look after you and the baby for a few minutes.'

'They said the baby's fine.' Cathy broke into fresh sobbing. 'She just won't have a father.'

Amy let her cry until the sobs subsided a little. Then she wiped her face gently with a damp towel. 'How's your pain level at the moment, Cathy? Do you need anything more for your elbow?'

'I don't care about my elbow.' Cathy stared at the

ceiling. 'What am I going to do?' she cried softly, not expecting an answer.

Amy used the next few minutes to assess Cathy. Her blood pressure and cardiac trace were good. The foetal monitor still attached to her abdomen also showed a steady heartbeat. Amy also rapidly perused the radiologist's report that had come back with Cathy's X-rays and the nursing notes made so far. Then she moved to check Cathy's splinted arm, concerned about the colour of her hand. As she did so, the curtain flicked back to admit a consultant. Amy had expected an orthopaedic surgeon to be called in. She hadn't expected it to be Nigel Wesley.

'What are you doing here?' she asked in surprise.

'I've come to see a patient. Is that a problem?' Nigel's tone was quiet but cutting, and Amy flushed.

'Of course not. I just didn't think your team was on call.'

'It's not. Fortunately I was still in the building and was available to help a colleague. Perhaps you'd like to stop blocking the viewing screen, Nurse Brooks, and allow me to get on with the job.'

Amy stepped sideways. She looked towards the head of the bed with concern but Cathy was still staring at the ceiling, oblivious to her surroundings. The news of Jack's death was still sinking in. Even if she could hear the conversation she would probably be uninterested. Amy wanted to get back to her and offer some support but Nigel was now blocking her access.

'What X-rays of the neck have been taken?'

Amy was glad she'd read the report. 'Anteroposterior, open-mouth odontoid and standard lateral and oblique views.'

Nigel snorted. 'I wouldn't call that a standard lateral view.'

'The radiologist felt that the loss of lordotic curve was within normal variations. He didn't think that flexion or extension laterals were called for at this stage. Neurological symptoms are confined to one side. He felt they were more likely to be due to the elbow injury than a cervical lesion. Read the report,' Amy suggested curtly. 'And you'll find the elbow X-rays there as well. Excuse me, but I want to get back to my patient.' She could hear Cathy crying again.

Nigel stepped backwards, blocking Amy again. 'Just a minute, Amy. I'd appreciate a better presentation of this case, if you don't mind. Just what are these unilateral neurological symptoms?'

Amy picked up the report. Janice had listed a limb baseline check twenty minutes ago. 'Cathy has pain, parathesia and paresis on the left side. Skin colour and temperature are slightly reduced, as is the pulse.'

'I think I need to know what the baselines are like now, not when you last bothered to fill in the report. At what times should baselines be taken?'

'Before and after splinting and every ten to fifteen minutes thereafter,' Amy responded acidly. Cathy's distress was cutting into her. How could Nigel act as though they were alone in the room? Was he completely inhuman? She would have to shove him physically to get past.

'And when were these baselines taken?'

'Twenty minutes ago.' Amy was ready to push Nigel.

'Not good enough, is it?' Nigel observed caustically. 'Just what have you been doing in here with your patient? Swapping recipes?'

Tom's entrance coincided with Nigel's sarcastic query. It was Amy he spoke to. 'We're ready for Cathy now.'

Nigel turned sharply at the sound of Tom's voice and Amy was able to brush past him without direct physical contact. She caught Cathy's hand.

'Tom's here now, Cathy. Would you like to talk to him or do you want to see Jack first?'

'I want to see Jack,' Cathy whispered. Tears rolled unchecked down her face.

Tom raised an eyebrow at Nigel who now stood at the end of the bed. 'Would you mind stepping out of the way?'

'You can't take this patient. I'm about to examine her.'

'Perhaps it can wait for a few minutes,' Tom suggested coldly. 'We're taking Cathy to see her husband. He died a short time ago.'

Nigel had the grace to look stunned. Silently he made way for the bed. Tom pushed it and Amy walked alongside, holding Cathy's hand tightly.

Jack had been moved to a side room devoid of high-tech equipment. The repair of his open chest wound had been done well enough to be invisible under the drape of clean linen. Jack's face had been relatively unmarked by the trauma and this was where Cathy reached out to touch him with her uninjured arm, as Tom and Amy positioned the beds alongside each other. They stayed in the room for a long time, quietly answering Cathy's questions and comforting her. Then they left at her request so that she could have a few minutes alone with her husband.

Amy glanced at Tom a little shyly. 'I don't think

I've ever seen a doctor handle something like that so well,' she told him.

'Part of the job,' Tom said casually. 'But I guess it helps to know what they're going through.'

Amy pondered Tom's tone. Did he mean he'd just had a lot of experience with patients' relatives? Or had he been through something traumatic himself? Amy wanted to know. Tom was always so cheerful. He was very skilled professionally, physically fit and active and very popular with staff and patients alike, but what did she really know about his personal life? Maybe sharing the experience they'd just had provided a good opportunity to ask.

The opportunity vanished. Nigel was pacing the floor of Resus 6.

'Just how long am I going to have to wait to see this patient?' he snapped.

'Don't let us keep you,' Tom said evenly. 'You're not even on call at present And I'm sure the patient load is under control by now. Why don't you just go home, Nigel?'

'Why don't you just mind your own business?' Nigel tone was venomous. 'I belong here more than you do,' he continued. 'And I have considerably more influence. I hope you're not setting your heart on getting this consultant position on a permanent basis.'

'That's my business,' Tom retorted. 'I'll take your advice and mind it carefully.'

Nigel seemed to take pleasure from the martyrdom of voluntary overtime after that exchange. He made a detailed examination of both Cathy's neck and elbow, ordering more X-rays and calling staff in for an out-of-hours MRI scan. He was still in the department at 9 p.m., when Cathy was due to be transferred to the

ward to wait for surgery in the morning. Amy found
him writing a report in Cathy's notes at the sorting desk
when she delivered another set of patient notes into the
outbasket. Tom was hanging up the telephone. He was
completely ignoring Nigel.

'So, Amy.' Tom's smile was warm. 'You are going
to come to the movies with me tomorrow night, aren't
you?'

Nigel snapped the notes shut and dropped the pen
onto the desk with a clatter. Amy's anger resurfaced
with a vengeance. His behaviour in Cathy's room had
been inexcusable from a professional point of view. It
was also inexcusable on a personal level. Amy wasn't
at fault this time. It had been Nigel who had stood her
up. Now he was angered by Tom's apparent confir-
mation of a date, was he?

'Sure, Tom,' Amy found herself saying. 'I'm looking forward to it.'

Nigel expelled a breath in what sounded like disgust
as he walked off. Amy caught Tom's eye.

'Not too keen on that idea, was he?' Tom murmured.

'No.' Amy caught her bottom lip between her teeth.
'Not very honest of me, is it?'

'What isn't?'

'Letting him think we have a date.'

'Why don't you come to the movies anyway?'

'I could,' Amy agreed. 'But it wouldn't be a *date*.'

Tom smiled. 'Doesn't really hurt to let Nigel think
it is, though, does it?'

Amy tried not to look as though the notion gave her
any pleasure. 'I guess not.'

'He doesn't need to know there's a whole group of
us going.'

'Is there?'

Tom nodded. 'It should be fun. Noel and Jen are coming and a few of the others. We'll go and have a drink first. Will you meet us at the pub?'

'Why not?' Amy pushed aside the momentary disappointment. She should feel relieved that there was a group going. As Tom had said, it should be fun.

Amy did enjoy the trip to the movies. She even enjoyed the session at the pub. Eyeing the table at which she'd sat alone and waited for Nigel, Amy decided to close that chapter of her life once and for all. She and Nigel were even. She'd humiliated him at the party and he'd returned the insult. He'd probably chosen this pub, knowing that her rejection was likely to be discovered by hospital staff and therefore made public.

If his behaviour yesterday during Cathy Hanson's traumatic admission to hospital was anything to go by, then Nigel's faults were a lot more than professional ego or a bad temper. His charm was purely superficial, probably insincere, and she was well out of it.

The evening meal at a Greek restaurant the following week was even better than the movies. Quite a large group of emergency department personnel attended and Amy was delighted when Tom chose to sit beside her.

'Anything special planned for your days off this week, angel?'

Amy shook her head and toyed with a calamari ring. Was Tom planning to ask her out? On a day when a group was unlikely to be mustered? 'I'll probably do some gardening if the weather's good,' she told Tom. 'It's a real mess. The roses haven't been pruned and all the summer flowers like delphiniums and foxgloves are being choked by weeds. I've been itching to get into it ever since winter.'

'You and Jen rent your place, don't you? Well, you must be the perfect tenants,' Tom observed. 'People usually only want to put the effort into something they own.'

'I'm not likely to own a garden for a long time,' Amy pointed out. She turned her attention back to her meal as Tom and Noel started discussing the times they could get together for a game of squash that week. Tom wasn't planning to ask her out. Why would he? She had made it very clear she wasn't prepared to go on anything that could be considered a date. She still wasn't. She needed time—and a new direction that was entirely her own, and Tom had given her an idea that kept her too preoccupied to even take much notice when the dancing started.

Restaurant staff and patrons snaked around the tables in a dance that involved little more than hanging onto the waist of the person in front. Amy resisted attempts to get her to join in and eventually everybody rejoined her for dessert. Janice reluctantly let go of Tom's waist and returned to her seat further up the table. Amy was ready to confide her idea.

'I think I'll buy a house,' she told Tom. 'You're right. I'd much rather put the effort into my own garden.'

'Good for you.' Tom smiled. 'Great minds think alike, angel. I'm house-hunting myself at the moment.'

'Really? Are you planning to stay in Christchurch?' Amy hoped she didn't sound as eager as she felt. 'Will you apply for the permanent position here, then?'

'I already have,' Tom said casually. 'But I don't know whether I'd take it. I'm just getting sick of the doctors' residence. I'll probably look for something to rent in the short term.'

Noel was trying to attract Tom's attention again. 'What about Wednesday *and* Friday for squash? I need the practice if I'm ever going to beat you.'

'Don't forget the tennis tournament on Saturday.' Janice had come around the table to lean over Amy's shoulder. 'We're in the doubles team.'

Amy laughed. 'Renting is probably the best idea for you, Tom. You'd never find the time to look after a garden.'

'What time is the tennis?' Tom asked. 'Only I've arranged to look at a house on Saturday morning. One of the O and G chaps told me about it.'

'One p.m.,' Noel responded. 'I should be through my ward round by 9.30. Do you want a second opinion on this house?'

'Absolutely.' Tom nodded.

'I'd better come, too, then,' Jennifer declared. 'Judging by Noel's flat, he has no taste in accommodation at all.'

Amy smiled a little wryly. Jennifer would know. She was spending a lot more time at Noel's flat than she was at home lately.

'I wish I could come.' Janice sounded disappointed. 'But I'm on all Friday night and if I don't get some sleep I might let you down in the tennis, Tom.'

'That would never do,' Tom agreed. 'Maybe Amy could come with us for another feminine viewpoint.'

Amy avoided meeting the stare she knew was coming from Janice. 'Sounds fun,' she said lightly. 'Count me in. I'm not on until Saturday afternoon.'

'You'll miss the tennis, then,' Janice informed her. 'What a shame.'

Amy just smiled. She wasn't as disappointed as Janice was pretending to be. She had another day to look forward to. Time away from work with her closest friends. Just the four of them. Her smile widened. It was almost a double date. Outside of professional situations it would be the closest she had been to spending time alone with Tom. That was, if you didn't count the meeting in the summer house before they'd even been introduced.

'We'll meet at the hospital, then,' Tom suggested. 'Eight-thirty OK?'

Noel and Jennifer nodded. Amy's nod was a little distracted. The thought of that meeting in the summer house had done all sorts of strange things to her physical equilibrium. She nodded again, more decisively. Eight-thirty was more than OK.

Definitely more than OK.

CHAPTER SIX

IT WAS 9 a.m. and Noel was nowhere in sight.

'I'll beep him,' Jennifer decided. 'He should have finished the ward round by now. I'll use the phone at the main reception desk.' She returned from making the call with a resigned expression.

'Noel can't make it,' she told Tom and Amy. 'The weasel's thrown a huge wobbly about one of the patients and he's insisting on taking her back to Theatre to realign her external fixation. It's not a huge job but she has to have a general anaesthetic and a theatre won't be available for at least half an hour.'

Tom checked his watch. 'We'd better go now or we won't be back in time for tennis. It's a bit of a drive over to Governers Bay, isn't it?'

'About twenty minutes,' Amy confirmed.

'Let's go, then,' Tom suggested. 'I don't mind making do with a totally feminine opinion.'

Jennifer looked uncomfortable. 'Noel asked me to meet him for a quick coffee while they're waiting for Theatre.' She smiled apologetically. 'I said I would.'

'My committee is deserting me,' Tom sighed.

'You and Amy could still go,' Jennifer urged.

Amy could feel Tom's watchful gaze. It settled on her face with a softness that belied the physical effect it engendered. Amy tried to ignore the shaft of sensation centred low in her abdomen. There would be no safety in numbers now. The double date had just halved. Was her reaction caused by nervousness...or excitement? Amy struggled to keep her expression non-chalant.

'I think Tom wanted more than just my opinion about this house, Jen. Couldn't you tell Noel you'll meet him later?'

'We'll make another time,' Tom cut in before Jennifer could respond. Amy's heart sank like a stone. Tom wasn't even hesitating in letting the opportunity to spend time alone with her pass. 'For you and Noel to see the place,' he continued smoothly. 'It's up to Amy. She's the chauffeur. What do you think, angel?' He touched her arm lightly, forcing her to meet his gaze directly.

'It's fine by me,' she agreed lightly. 'It's a lovely morning for a drive.'

It was a lovely morning. The bright sunlight was only dimmed by the thickness of the pine plantation they drove through as they followed the road leading from the suburb of Cashmere and winding its way to the summit of the Port Hills. The force of the light struck with renewed clarity as they emerged to a view of the city and plains, bordered by the Southern Alps in the far distance. Tom drew in his breath at the sight.

'I never appreciated how beautiful this city is,' he said in wonder. 'I was too young when I left.'

'Just wait.' Amy smiled. 'We're almost at the top. It's the best bit.'

She slowed the car as they reached the apex of the road. With a startling contrast the view of the city and mountains was forgotten as the clear blue of the har-bour and the flowing greenery of the peninsula hills and islands was suddenly spread before them. Smiling again at Tom's stunned expression, Amy kept her speed down. The descent of the road on this side was steep and curvy and it was a favourite route for serious cyclists. Tom eyed a Lycra-clad couple who looked as though they had stayed on their cycles the whole way up.

'I could bike to work,' he mused. 'That would keep me fit.'

Amy laughed. 'Certainly would. I wouldn't fancy it in the middle of winter myself. It snows up here quite often.' She changed gears to negotiate a sharp turn. 'It's a fair way out of town, really. Are you sure it would suit you?'

'You seem to have doubts that it would.' Tom wasn't watching the scenery any more. Amy felt the familiar touch of his gaze. 'Why is that?'

Amy was glad she needed to keep her eyes on the road. 'I guess you seem to be a social creature. You like being in a crowd. Parties and tennis matches and so on. Always something happening and lots of people to share it with.'

Tom was silent for a moment. 'I guess I would give that impression.' His tone became more thoughtful. 'But first impressions can be misleading. Maybe there aren't many people I'd want to be alone with.'

Amy had to change the subject. 'Did you ever go out to that big island when you were a kid?'

'Never. I don't even know what it's called.' Tom obediently transferred his gaze to the nearest island in the harbour.

'It's Quail Island. It has quite a history.' Amy's confidence increased as she escaped the dangerously personal conversation. 'It got farmed for a while by the Ward family around 1850, but two of the brothers got drowned in the harbour. Then it became a quarantine station and even had a leper colony on it for a long time. They used prisoners from the Lyttelton jail to build walls and jetties and plant trees. The hospital was used during the flu epidemic in 1918.'

'How do you know so much about it?' Tom sounded impressed.

'Just interested, I guess. And I like reading.'

'What else do you like, Amy?'

'Driving,' Amy responded promptly. 'Getting out of the city for a while. I often go for a long drive on my days off,' she confided. 'I take some lunch and a good book for when I find a nice place to stop.'

'Sounds lonely.'

Amy turned left as they reached the bottom of the hill. Glimpses of Quail Island continued as she drove around the harbour coast. She searched for an easy way to break the silence that had fallen after Tom's quiet comment.

'When Antarctic exploration really got under way after the turn of the century, they quarantined dogs and ponies on Quail Island.' Amy knew she was sounding like a guidebook. Tom's smile suggested he was aware of the reason the island was still being used as a conversation piece.

'Really?'

'Mmm.' Amy tried to sound as though the subject had fascinated her for a long time. 'They used the beach to train the animals to pull heavy loads. Christchurch still has strong Antarctic connections.' Amy pulled to the side of the road as they reached a small bay. 'Where's that list of directions again? I think the turn-off must be quite close.'

Amy turned off the main road a short time later onto what looked like a cart track leading into a heavily treed patch of hillside.

'I hope this is the right place,' she said dubiously. 'I can't even see a house.'

'The name on the letter-box was right.' Tom sounded confident. 'Mike said it was well tucked away.'

'He wasn't kidding.' When Amy climbed out of the car she stood and gazed about her in wonder. The dark green stain of the house timbers and the weathered wooden shingles of the roof made it blend into the dense grove of large old trees. The silence was almost complete. A breeze from the harbour stirred the trees into a whispering background for myriad bird calls. Sunshine filtered down, dappling the mossy brick pathway they were standing on.

'This is amazing,' Amy whispered. 'I can't wait to see inside.'

'Come on, then.' Tom led the way to a heavy wooden door. Light from within the house lit up a round stained-glass window set into it. Amy waited for Tom to use the old iron door-knocker, but instead he produced a key from his pocket and inserted it into the lock.

'Mike let me have a key,' he explained in response to Amy's raised eyebrows. 'They're away for the week, house-hunting in Auckland.'

So it wasn't just the drive that Amy was to be alone with Tom for. Now they were shut away from the world with a forest cottage to explore together. Amy took a deep breath and stepped over the threshold, and found herself in one of the most beautiful rooms she had ever seen. The house appeared to be two-storied from the outside but Amy now discovered the vaulted cathedral ceiling that took in the whole height of the dwelling. The ceiling and supporting beams were all of rich, native timber. Two wooden staircases ran to mezzanine floors on three sides of the room and Amy gazed around in delight as she realised the cleverness of the design.

The house had no real interior walls but was divided into quite intimate areas by the use of different levels. They stepped down a small flight of polished wooden stairs into a sitting room, the focus of which was a pot-bellied stove set into an elaborately tiled antique fire surround. Raised from the central sunken area at one end was a television and music centre. At the other end, a dining alcove led out onto a flagged terrace and adjoined a modern kitchen with windows that gave the same view of the harbour and islands that could be seen from the terrace.

The only trees which had been trimmed were those that impeded the view, and even that attention had been minimal. The height of the house and the slope of the hill it was built on allowed an almost unrestricted panorama and ample sunshine to enter the building. They could have been a hundred miles away from the city, as no other houses could be seen. Amy sighed with pleasure.

'This is absolutely stunning, Tom. I've never seen anything like it.'

'Come on, let's see the rest.'

Amy followed Tom up the stairs to the mezzanine floor. The vaulted ceiling sloped over them and they were protected from the drop by wooden railings. She realised that the house was actually quite small, it was just the design that gave such an impression of size. The divisions upstairs were highlighted by differently shaped stained-glass windows. An archway-shaped window gave the library and study area a calm atmosphere and the round glass decorated with a nautical theme fitted well with the bathroom. It could be seen over the heavy wooden bookshelves that provided the division and screening for the room.

'The house is for sale.' Tom was gazing over the railing into the body of the house. 'If I rent it, it will only be available until they find a buyer.'

'It could be difficult to leave.' Amy smiled. 'I couldn't imagine a more perfect place to live.'

Tom held her gaze, his expression serious. Then it changed, with one of those instant shifts that Amy found fascinating. His eyes danced as he smiled. 'One more room to see.'

It seemed completely natural to accept the invitation of the extended hand. And to keep holding it as they moved past another screen made of large old wooden storage cupboards. A picture window gave a view not of the harbour but of trees at the back of the property surrounding a tiny green lawn and garden. The iron bedstead fitted snugly against one wall, the patchwork of the quilt seeming to bring the greenery of the outside trees into the room. Still holding hands, Amy stood at the window with Tom. She opened her mouth to comment on the garden but the unspoken words died as she turned to discover just how close to her Tom was standing. He wasn't looking at the view at all.

Silently, Tom let go of Amy's hand and raised his own to brush a finger softly along the outline of her jaw. Mesmerised, Amy allowed herself to sink into the depths of his gaze as he slowly cupped her chin and tilted her head back. Then his eyes were too close to focus on. Instead, Amy could feel the whisper of his breath on her face. On her lips.

Alcohol must have dampened the sensation of that

first kiss in the summer house. Either that, or her fantasies had been unable to capture the magic of the touch. This kiss was nothing like the first one. It was nothing like anything Amy had ever experienced in her whole life. Instinctively, her hands went to Tom's face, needing to touch the source of such exquisite pleasure. At the silken slide of his tongue against hers, Amy pushed her fingers into his soft, dark hair, pulling his face closer, her lips parting to beg for more.

She could feel Tom's hands stroke firmly down the outline of her body on both sides. As they reached her hips, his thumbs pressed deeply down the inside of her hip bones and Amy shuddered with the overwhelming wave of desire the contact provoked. Arching back, she found they were touching in a way that left her in no doubt about Tom's reaction to the kiss. He wanted her as much as she wanted him.

Tom's hands moved again, this time to unbutton the silk shirt Amy was wearing. They brushed the soft swell of her breasts and Amy gasped at the painfully sweet prickle as her nipples hardened instantaneously. Tom's hands were still moving. He was undoing the fastening of her jeans. Amy wanted to be rid of her clothes. She wanted Tom to touch her breasts, to slide his hands over her hips again. To feel her legs against his without the distraction of any barriers.

It was the thought of Tom touching her legs—*seeing* her legs—that broke the spell. Amy struggled to gain enough control to step back.

'What's wrong, Amy?'

She ignored the gentle query, turning away to stuff the tail of her shirt back into place and refasten the buttons.

'Amy?' Tom's tone was firmer. 'Talk to me.'

She fumbled the last button. 'I don't want this, Tom.' In the silence that followed, Amy waited for the accusation that she could have fooled him. He would have been quite justified in making it.

'Because of Nigel?'

'No. Nigel has nothing to do with this.' Amy moved, holding the hand rail as she descended the staircase. She waited in silence as Tom locked the door behind them.

'I think Nigel has quite a lot to do with this,' he suggested.

Amy was silent. Maybe it would be easier to let Tom believe that explanation.

Tom caught hold of Amy's arm. 'I want you, Amy. You know that.'

'You don't know anything about me,' Amy countered. She pulled away and got into the car, starting the engine before Tom had followed suit. She glanced at her passenger as he fastened his seat belt, expecting Tom to look annoyed at her dismissal. But he was smiling.

'I know you like reading,' he reminded her. 'And you like driving.' He raised his eyebrows as they reached the tarmac of the main road and Amy put her foot down. Tom remained silent as Amy took the little car through the curves of the summit road with all the skill of a rally driver.

'You like driving fast,' he commented casually when they finally slowed to enter the outskirts of the city. He grinned lopsidedly. 'I'm pleased to say you're also very good at it.'

'Thanks.'

'You're very good at your job, too.'

'Thanks.' Amy smiled ruefully. 'I'm sure Nigel Wesley wouldn't agree with you.'

'I'm sure Nigel and I wouldn't agree on a lot of things,' Tom said coolly. 'Including you.' He paused. 'We're still friends, aren't we, Amy? I haven't scared you off?'

Amy hesitated. 'No,' she said cautiously, with a sidelong glance. 'Just so long as we both know what the boundaries of friendship are.'

'No-go areas,' Tom agreed. 'For now.'

Amy nodded. This was familiar territory. Set boundaries. Keep a relationship going as long as possible without having to reveal the truth. Hope it might grow into something that could survive the truth. Except that, this time, it felt completely wrong. The silence that fell between them grew steadily more uncomfortable.

'Pull over for a minute, Amy,' Tom ordered suddenly.

Amy complied. 'Are you feeling car sick?' she asked anxiously. 'I drove too fast, didn't I?'

'No. I just want to talk to you.'

'Oh.' Amy pulled to the side of the road and cut the engine. She kept her hands resting on the steering-wheel, her eyes fixed on the passing traffic.

'I said I'd help you get a life, didn't I?' Tom reminded Amy. 'To let you see that there was more to life than Nigel Wesley.'

Amy nodded, still watching the traffic.

'We've had fun, haven't we?'

Amy nodded yet again. She wouldn't like to confess how much she would miss spending time in Tom's company.

'It doesn't have to stop, Amy. Come out with me.

We'll do something completely different. I'll take you dancing and I promise I won't kiss you.'

'I don't dance,' Amy said miserably.

'Only because you don't know how to. I'll teach you.'

'No.' Amy took a deep breath. 'I don't mean I don't know how to dance. Or that I don't want to dance. I mean I can't.'

'Why not?'

Amy hesitated for a long, awkward moment. 'It's just that…that some things are a bit more difficult for me,' she confessed finally.

'Things like ice skating?' Tom suggested. 'And tennis?'

Amy nodded. 'And bike riding and tramping. I'm really not sporty, Tom.'

'What's the problem? Have you got a tin leg?'

Amy laughed and then bit her lip. 'Just about,' she admitted. 'I had a bad accident when I was a kid. One leg is shorter than the other one.'

'Gets a bit sore when you're tired, doesn't it?' Tom sympathised.

'You've noticed that?' Amy asked, surprised.

'I've seen you, once or twice, trying not to limp.' Tom sounded matter-of-fact. 'And you get blue shadows under your eyes if you're in pain.'

Amy swallowed. He'd been watching her *that* closely?

'What happened?' Tom asked.

'I got shot when I was ten. My femur was shattered by a high-powered rifle bullet.'

'Good grief!' Tom exclaimed. 'What on earth were you doing?'

'I was out hunting with my father. Deer-shooting up in the ranges.'

Tom stared at her. 'I can't see it. Angels don't go around killing deer.'

'I couldn't see it either. That was the problem.' Amy sighed deeply. 'I told you my father wanted a son. All he got was me, so he decided he'd better make the best of a bad situation and teach me to do boy stuff. I hated anything to do with guns so I sneaked off into the hills and got mistaken for a deer.'

'It was your *father* who accidentally shot you?'

Amy nodded. Tom was silent for a moment. Then he touched Amy's hand. 'Do the things that are more difficult for you include getting undressed in broad daylight?'

Amy sounded miserable. 'I'm sorry, Tom.'

He ignored the apology, his eyes narrowing slightly. 'I imagine Nigel said something to upset you, did he? When he saw your leg?'

'He's never seen it,' Amy confessed. 'He only knows I don't like anyone seeing it.'

'You mean you only got undressed in the dark,' Tom said. He was staring at Amy as she reddened. 'You didn't get undressed?' he asked incredulously. Then he grinned. 'How did you manage that?'

Amy was acutely embarrassed. 'We never went that far,' she snapped. 'It's not some sort of joke, Tom Barlow. Not everyone wants to leap into bed on the first date.'

'Certainly true when it comes to Nigel, I expect.' Tom was still grinning. 'Don't get mad, Amy. This is me you're talking to. I'm your friend, remember? I'm helping you to get a life. I'm taking you dancing.'

'No, you're not.' Amy found his persistence staggering. 'I've just explained—'

'Listen, Amy,' Tom interrupted. 'You've got a hang-up about your leg. I think you need to push the boundaries a bit. You cope with a demanding physical job. I've watched you. There's no reason why you couldn't cope with having fun with your body as well. Just try it,' he added persuasively. 'If it's a problem, we'll stop. If you don't try, you'll never know what you might have been missing out on, will you?'

'I suppose not,' Amy admitted reluctantly. 'But being able to dance isn't that important.'

'Being able to live is. Knowing what you're capable of doing is. Knowing that barriers you've put up don't actually need to be there is probably quite important, don't you think?'

Amy sighed. 'You're pushy, you know that?'

'I know.' Tom's grin was cheeky. 'But you'll come dancing with me?'

'Not if you're going with a whole crowd. I have no intention of making a public spectacle of myself.'

'No crowds, I promise. Just you and me.' Tom turned to gaze innocently out of the window after Amy finally nodded her acceptance. 'I'm not sure about keeping that other promise, however.'

'What other promise?'

'The one about not kissing you.'

'Oh.' Amy bit back her smile as she started the car up again. 'I guess I'll just have to see if I can cope.' She indicated her return to the stream of traffic. 'If I don't try I'll never know what I might be missing out on, will I?'

CHAPTER SEVEN

THE dancing lesson had to wait.

Amy had two days of afternoon duties that ran from 11 a.m. to 10 p.m. Then she was rostered for two days of an earlier shift that finished at 6 p.m. After that, she could look forward to four days off. The afternoon duties on Saturday and Sunday passed in a haze of anticipation, the likes of which she had never previously experienced.

Tom knew about her leg. And he still wanted her. Not the way Nigel had, with that undertone of it being a little less than acceptable but something he was noble enough to overlook. Tom didn't see it as a barrier to anything—even dancing. Maybe she would be able to do it with that sort of encouragement. Amy had never even entertained the possibility that she could attempt a physical activity such as dancing, but Tom was right. She coped with a demanding job in physical terms— she'd learned how to cope through her determination to succeed. She'd simply not allowed her leg to keep her from the career she loved. What if she applied the same attitude to other challenges? Like dancing?

Even a small boy with the head of a decapitated plastic soldier up his nose wouldn't have irritated Amy that weekend. Patients came and went through the emergency department in a typical stream of minor to major illnesses and injuries, covering the whole spectrum of distress levels. Those fortunate enough to be treated by Amy all left feeling much happier. Gareth

119

was available when one such patient was discharged from Amy's care.

The teenage girl had been brought in by ambulance, suffering a severe hypoglycaemic episode. She'd forgotten her morning dose of insulin and had tried to make up for it by doubling her evening dose. The treatment of IV glucose administration had already been done by the ambulance crew, and for Amy the nursing care had involved monitoring the blood-sugar levels, support through the confused state of regaining full consciousness and the persuasion needed to get her patient to eat both some short-acting and long-acting carbohydrates. Amy had gone to the kitchen to make a sandwich for the girl herself. The mother had gone to Gareth Harvey before they'd left the department.

'I don't care what they say about the problems in the health system these days. The nurse who has been looking after my daughter is simply wonderful.'

Gareth told Amy about the woman's praise a little later. 'Perhaps that nickname of ''angel'' isn't misplaced,' he observed with a smile.

Amy blushed. How had the head of the emergency department picked up on Tom's name for her?

'I must say you're looking happy, Amy,' Gareth added. 'It's good to see.'

Amy was happy. She'd never felt happier. Imagine being able to *dance*.

To dance with *Tom*.

Expecting to have to wait until Wednesday before Tom would make arrangements for their date, Amy's level of anticipation went up several notches on Tuesday morning.

'You finish at 6 p.m., don't you, angel?'

'I hope so.'

'Then let's go out tonight. I should finish by then, too.' Tom's gaze was enfolding Amy in a delicious warmth. 'You won't be too tired, will you?'

'No.' Amy dropped her gaze. 'I'm looking forward to it.'

Tom bent his head closer to hers. 'Good. Because you're going to love it, Amy. I promise.'

Amy found it difficult to concentrate on her work with Tom in the department. Every time she caught sight of him she thought of his promises. She knew she was going to love dancing. The mere thought of standing still with Tom's arms around her was enough to sent her pulse rate up. The prospect of their bodies moving closely together, touching, was…was interfering with her work, that's what it was.

Peter must have noticed that Amy wasn't operating with her usual effectiveness. He called her over to the sorting desk.

'We're short-staffed in the EOA, Amy. Would you mind spending the rest of your shift in there today?'

'Not at all.' Amy would normally have considered time away from the sharp end of emergency medical care a type of punishment. She went quite willingly today. She wouldn't see Tom as frequently and wouldn't work with him directly, but that was probably a good idea right now. She wouldn't have to be so distracted. And she could stop thinking about that other promise. The one he had no intention of keeping. The one about not kissing her again.

Assigned five patients to care for in the emergency observation area, Amy was kept busy, monitoring her patients' conditions, collating results on tests and assisting with examinations as various specialists were called in for assessment. The general surgical registrar came in for a second visit to one her patients, a forty-five-year-old solicitor by the name of Stephen Parks.

'The ultrasound has confirmed what we suspected, Stephen. We need to take your appendix out. I've got a consent form here for you to sign and we've got you lined up for Theatre in an hour or so.'

'Can't it wait for a while?'

'I wouldn't advise it.'

'But I've got a major case on. I'm due in court tomorrow.' Stephen Parks shifted uncomfortably. 'It's grumbled before. A few painkillers and I'll be fine.'

'I'm afraid it's a bit more serious this time. If an appendix gets swollen enough it can rupture, in which case it sends infected material all over the place. You can get very seriously ill with peritonitis.'

'You'd end up being in hospital a lot longer if that happened, Stephen,' Amy pointed out. 'This way, you'll only be in for a night or two. You could be back at work by next week.'

The registrar's beeper sounded. He looked questioningly at Stephen who shook his head. The doctor pulled back the curtain. 'I'll have to answer my beeper. Excuse me.'

Janice walked past the bed, carrying a toddler. She smiled at the registrar. Amy stepped away from the bed, stretching out her hand.

'Leave the consent form with me. I'll have another word with Stephen while you're answering your call.'

Stephen looked keen to talk as Amy returned. He was sitting up much straighter in bed. 'Who was that nurse who just walked past with the baby? The one with dark hair?'

'Her name's Janice,' Amy told him. 'Janice Healey.'

Stephen settled back against his pillows. 'Maybe I

will stick around for a bit longer. I can always get an adjournment on my case. Give me that consent form to have a look at.' He winked at Amy. 'And leave the curtain open, will you?'

Janice had delivered the toddler and his parents to another bed in the EOA and was leaving as Amy helped elderly Mrs Turner to the toilet. Stephen raised his hand as Janice went past his bed.

'Excuse me. Janice, is it?'

Janice paused, surprised. 'Yes?'

Stephen's smile was appealing. 'Could you possibly find me a glass of water?'

'He's nil by mouth,' Amy warned. 'Mr Parks might be off to Theatre shortly.'

'I'm sorry,' Amy heard Janice apologise. 'You're not allowed anything to drink at the moment. Mr Parks, is that your name?'

'Stephen,' the patient corrected firmly. 'Call me Stephen, Janice.'

Amy shook her head but couldn't be irritated even by Janice's eager response to the male attention. It wasn't Janice Tom was taking dancing tonight, was it?

Activity in the EOA decreased as the day wore on. Several staff members were on their lunch-break when Stephen Parks was wheeled off to Theatre, and Amy was aware of a peaceful lull. She tidied up Stephen's area. The curtains had been disrupted by the removal of the bed and Amy found she was being observed by a young man in the next bed. He had a very friendly face and his smile was instantly attractive. Amy smiled back.

'Do you want this curtain closed again?' The patient was still screened from general view. It was only the side curtain which had been inadvertently pulled open.

Amy didn't know this patient and he might well have
requested solitude for some reason.

'No, thanks. It's nice to see someone. I'm getting a
bit bored.'

'Perhaps you'd like the other curtain opened?' Amy
suggested. 'You could see what's going on, then.'

'No. I'd rather forget where I am. Why don't you
come and distract me for a minute?'

The patient looked about the same age as Amy. The
gentle tone of his voice was as attractive as his smile.

Amy returned the smile. She stepped closer. 'I could
call your nurse for you, if you like.'

'No. I'd rather talk to you. What's your name?'

'Amy Brooks.'

'Pleased to meet you, Amy.' He held out his wrist,
adorned with a hospital identification bracelet. 'I'm
Jason,' he introduced himself.

Amy touched his wrist, turning the plastic strap towards her. Jason Andrew Kingsley, the information
stated, along with his hospital number and date of birth.

'Twenty-fourth of August!' Amy exclaimed. 'That's
my birthday. It's even the same year.'

'I knew we had something in common.' Jason's
smile flashed again. 'I would have picked you for a
Virgo, anyway.'

'Really?' Amy dismissed the thought that she was
as bad as Janice, responding to a male patient's friendly
overture. It really was a little unprofessional, letting a
patient hold her hand like this, but Amy excused herself by using the moment to assess Jason. He was rather
too thin and pale but didn't appear to be in any distress.
His hair was short. Extremely short. It crossed Amy's
mind that he might have had recent surgery or drug
therapy which had resulted in dramatic hair loss. Her

attention was caught more by his eyes than anything else. Maybe the hair loss accentuated them. Or maybe it was because they were brown and reminded her of Tom Barlow.

'You look efficient and gentle,' Jason informed her. Amy ducked her head. *He* wasn't going to say she looked like an angel, was he? Jason rubbed his thumb along her fourth finger. 'No rings, then?'

'No.' Amy extracted her hand gently. This was getting decidedly unprofessional. 'I'd better go, Jason. I've got patients to look after.'

'Look after me.' Jason grinned. 'The nurse I've got looks like a real battleaxe.'

Amy hid her smile. Jason's nurse had to be Sheila. The older woman's appearance was daunting but didn't really disguise the fact that she was an excellent nurse.

'You, however, look like an angel.'

'Yeah, right.' Amy rolled her eyes. Funny how that word could affect her so instantly now. It had always been a joke until Tom had picked it up and used it for a nickname. 'Have you got any visitors coming, Jason?'

'Only my parents. Nobody special,' Jason told her forlornly. He grinned again. 'What are you doing after work?'

They both laughed. As Amy turned away, Jason's laughter stopped abruptly. Surprised, Amy glanced back to see Jason's eyes fluttering shut. Suddenly alarmed, Amy picked up his wrist and felt for a pulse.

Nothing.

She placed a hand on his neck, leaning close to check for respiration at the same time.

Still nothing.

This couldn't be happening. To have someone as

young as Jason Kingsley talking and laughing one minute and then in cardiac and respiratory arrest seconds later. Amy knocked the bed flat and hauled out the pillows. She pushed the cardiac-arrest alarm button on the wall. The first help to arrive was Jason's nurse, Sheila, who was pushing the arrest trolley. The older nurse stopped as she saw Amy with Jason's head tilted back, a hand positioned around his chin, the other pinching his nostrils closed as she inflated his lungs, her lips pressed firmly over his. Amy hadn't waited even the few seconds it would have taken to locate an oral airway and bag mask.

'Oh, *no!*'

Amy could understand Sheila's horrified tone. This was an unexpected and catastrophic complication with her patient. What she couldn't understand was that her colleague was standing motionless, making no attempt to assist her efforts.

'For God's sake, Sheila. Charge up the defibrillator. Start compressions. Don't just *stand* there!'

'I can't. Amy—you musn't!'

Amy finished her second breath for Jason and leaned over him. With the heel of one hand pressed onto the back of the other she began to compress his chest, counting swiftly and silently until she reached fifteen. Another breath was due. Amy was unaware of the man standing behind her until he touched her.

'You have to stop, Amy. This is a ''no resuscitation'' case.'

'What?' Amy's head snapped around to find Tom watching her. Her gaze flew back to Jason. His lips were turning blue.

'Are you crazy?' Amy was almost shouting. 'He's only twenty-nine!'

Tom looked calm. Sympathetic but in control. He caught hold of Amy's wrist as she tried to reposition her hands for more compressions.

'Amy, *no!*' he said sternly.

Amy stared at Tom's face. She saw no hint of the shock she was feeling. No desire to try and save a gentle young man who had been talking and laughing only minutes ago. What Amy saw was a determination to prevent her from making any attempt to save Jason's life. Other staff members had gathered. She recognised one of the cardiology registrars. Amy could see expressions of pity—even embarrassment. She wrenched her wrist from Tom's grasp, pushed blindly past him and through the curtains. Amy broke into a run as she cleared the EOA. She kept moving until she left the building and still she didn't stop. She was instinctively heading for the solitude of the river that wound through the hospital grounds.

It was Tom who found Amy, over an hour later, sitting hunched on a bench seat. She was shivering and her eyes were red from tears she still couldn't stifle completely.

'Oh, Amy.' Tom sat down beside her and folded her into his arms. 'It's all right, sweetheart.'

Amy pushed him away. 'How can it be all right?' she cried. 'How could you have done that? Just let him *die!*' Another hiccup of a sob escaped her.

'Amy, listen.' Tom sounded very sombre. 'Jason Kingsley had a form of acute myeloid leukaemia. In the last six months he's failed all possible avenues of treatment and the prognosis was extremely limited. One of the drugs he was having in the chemotherapy caused him to go into a degree of heart failure. He was in the EOA waiting for a bed in CCU to become available. The cardiologists were going to assess him to see if the quality of life he had could be improved for the few weeks or possibly months he had remaining. It was his—very firm—request that he not be resuscitated if the situation arose. He had the legal documentation needed and the staff involved agreed that he had perfectly reasonable grounds to make the request and that they would comply.' Tom was looking at the river as he spoke. His tone seemed detached, as though he were reading a written statement.

Amy's brow furrowed. 'What about bone-marrow transplant?'

'He had everything. Course after course of chemotherapy with three or more cytotoxic drugs at a time. Total marrow irradiation and transplant from his mother who had the closest tissue match.'

Tom's tone was disturbing Amy. 'He's just another patient to you, isn't he?' she accused. 'You don't seem to care very much. He must have been through hell.'

'Yes.' The direct gaze Amy received now was as distant as his tone. 'And not just from the treatments. His white cell count was so bad he was prone to every infection and he seemed to catch them all. Skin infections, septicaemia and two lots of pneumonia—the second of which almost killed him last month. He'd had enough, Amy, can you understand that?'

'Of course I can.' Amy felt alarmed by the sudden change she detected in Tom. Had she committed enough of a professional error to turn him against her? Did he now think there might be some truth in Nigel's assessment of her competence? 'I should have been told,' she added quietly.

'Of course you should. That was an oversight on the

part of the EOA staff. Maybe they forgot because you don't normally work in that area. They were under stress as well, being so short-staffed.'

'It was very unprofessional of me, wasn't it?' Amy bit her lip. 'I was shouting. I must have upset everybody. It's just that he was so lovely and we'd been laughing together. He even asked me what I was doing after work and then…'

'It was an upsetting case. They understand.' Tom touched Amy's arm. 'I understand.'

Amy searched his face. The flicker of warmth *was* still there. It was just buried under something she didn't quite recognise. Sadness? Or possibly wariness. Was he wary of her potential over-emotional tendency?

'I'm ready to go back now,' Amy told him. 'I'm sorry I caused so much trouble.'

'You don't have to apologise.' Tom stood up and Amy followed suit. 'You don't have to go back either, if you don't feel up to it. Gareth said to tell you to take the rest of the shift off if you needed some space.'

'I'll be fine.' Amy tried to sound confident. 'I don't want to miss work.'

They walked back to the main building together.

'What about tonight, Amy? Do you want to give our dancing lesson a miss?''

'No.' Amy tried to smile. 'It's probably just what I need.'

Tom's smile seemed automatic. 'I've got a meeting at 5.30. How 'bout I meet you in the car park at 6.30? I'll take you home to get changed and then we'll head out.'

'Sounds great.' Amy took a deep breath. 'And thanks for coming to find me, Tom. Goodness knows how long I might have sat there otherwise.'

'You would have come back.' Tom's smile had its usual warmth again. 'I just didn't want to wait that long.'

The clocks finally reached 6 p.m. and Amy left the department ten minutes later with an uncharacteristic sense of relief. It had been a roller-coaster of a day for her and she felt emotionally drained. Thanks to her headlong flight away from the scene of Jason Kingsley's death, her leg also ached badly. The excited anticipation with which she'd looked forward to the dancing lesson had ebbed dramatically. Now Amy had real doubts that she could cope. Physically or emotionally. A postponement might be a very good idea.

Amy sat down on the stone wall bordering the car park. She had twenty minutes to wait. If the rest didn't do something to help the pain she would definitely have to call off the date. Ten minutes' rest didn't make any difference to her level of discomfort. The appearance of Nigel in the car park made the situation even less tolerable. Amy wished she'd noticed the bottle green BMW earlier. She could have chosen somewhere else to sit. Anywhere else.

'Not waiting for me, are you, Amy?' Nigel's eyebrows were raised sardonically. There was no hint of any smile.

'No.' Amy avoided eye contact. 'I'm waiting for someone else.'

'Let me guess,' Nigel said unpleasantly. 'It wouldn't be Tom Barlow, by any chance, would it?'

Amy was silent.

Nigel jingled his car keys in his hand. 'It wouldn't surprise me in the least. Not since I heard you stood me up to go out with him.'

Amy was stung into responding. '*You* stood *me* up, Nigel. I waited in that pub for over an hour.'

'What pub?' Nigel snarled. 'The arrangement was to meet at Two Six Four.'

Amy blinked. Two Six Four was the street number and name of one of the more exclusive restaurants in the city. Certainly more Nigel's style than the local pub. 'Laura wouldn't have made a mistake like that,' she said cautiously.

'Who actually *gave* you the message, Amy?'

Amy tried to dismiss a cold feeling of dread. There had to be an explanation for this.

'Was it Tom Barlow?' Nigel queried coldly.

Amy nodded slowly. What was going on here?

'I might have known.' Nigel turned and took several angry paces before swinging sharply back to face Amy. 'Can't you see what's going on here?'

'No.'

Nigel took a step closer. 'We were perfectly happy before Tom Barlow showed up. We still could be. I don't leave for Sydney for two weeks. We could sort this out if it wasn't for Barlow.' Nigel shook his head incredulously. 'He's determined to destroy what we had. And you're going to let him succeed.'

'Don't be ridiculous, Nigel.' Amy was disgusted by the accusation. 'Why the hell would he want to do that?'

'Why don't you ask him yourself?'

Amy tore her stare away from Nigel to see Tom walking towards them. When he spotted Nigel talking to her, his face set into grim lines. By the time he reached the pair he looked distant, under control only by withdrawal. Much the same as he'd looked when telling Amy about Jason Kingsley's history. Amy's sense of dread returned to lodge like a boulder in her stomach.

'Did you deliberately give me the wrong message about where I was supposed to meet Nigel that night, Tom?' Amy's question came out far more coherently than she'd expected, but Tom made no response. 'I could easily check with Laura. She would remember.'

Tom gave a resigned sigh. 'All right, Amy. Yes, I did change the message.'

'Why?'

'Because you needed protection from Nigel. You had no idea what you might be getting into.'

'And you did?' Amy was still grappling with the fact that it had been Tom who set her up, not Nigel.

'He's not good enough for you.'

Nigel snorted contemptuously. 'And you are? Just who's lying and cheating now, Barlow?' Nigel sounded smug. 'It's not you he wants, Amy. He's just trying to get at me.'

Amy stared at Nigel. 'You're mad. He's only been in the country for a few weeks. He doesn't even know you.'

'Oh, but I do, Amy,' Tom said heavily. 'I've known Nigel Wesley all my life.'

Amy shifted the direction of her stare towards Tom. She didn't even blink. 'How?'

'We share the same father.'

Amy still hadn't blinked. 'You're *brothers*?'

'*Half*-brothers,' Tom corrected icily.

'Still enough for you to think you have the right to interfere with my life.' Nigel's lip curled. 'You always have. You stole my inheritance, Barlow. You stole my woman.'

'I haven't been *stolen*.' Amy was humiliated to be discussed as though she were some kind of possession.

'Perhaps I'm not talking about you.' Nigel didn't spare Amy a glance. 'Perhaps you're not the first.'

'That was all a very long time ago, Nigel.' Tom shook his head wearily. 'You've never been able to move on, have you? Obsession is one of your many faults.'

'And you move on so easily, don't you? Countries, jobs, *women*.' Nigel almost spat the last word. Now he did look directly at Amy. 'Ask him what sort of commitment he's capable of, Amy.' Nigel's smile was ruthless. 'Ask him about his *wife*. That didn't last very long either, did it?'

Amy could feel the colour drain from her face. The solid weight in her stomach became a painful cramp. 'You're married, Tom?' The words came out in a hoarse whisper.

'I was.' Tom's admission was devoid of expression.

'Didn't last long, did it?' Nigel taunted.

'No.' A single word. It hung in the air, almost visible in the silence that followed it.

Nigel broke the silence. 'It's not me you need protection from, Amy. It's him. I think I'd better take you home.'

The pain was total. Physical and emotional. It was unbearable. Amy looked at each of the two men standing in front of her. Nigel was first.

'No, thanks, Nigel.' Amy eased herself off the wall. 'I really don't think I want anything more to do with you.'

Tom got her attention just before she summoned the reserves to walk away.

'*Either* of you.'

CHAPTER EIGHT

THE pieces slotted together as neatly as any jigsaw puzzle.

Amy clambered to her feet and stretched her back cautiously. Four days spent largely attacking the garden had taken its toll on underused muscles and joints. Four days of endless introspection had taken its toll as well. Amy was mentally and emotionally drained. There was nothing left. Just a vast and dark emptiness and the painful comprehension of how it had occurred.

Amy bent over again, ignoring the sharp twinge in her leg. She scooped up the last armful of pruned foliage and weeds to ferry the rubbish to the impressive compost heap she had created. She paused for a moment to survey the results of her efforts. The garden was completely in order. Roses and shrubs had been pruned to a shape they hadn't known for years. Not a single weed was visible. Even the lawn edges boasted a military neatness.

Like Nigel's beard. Amy sighed wearily. Why couldn't she stop the endless spin of her thoughts? They always settled into the same pattern. A pattern that was now as neatly ordered as this garden. Nigel had to be right. Tom hadn't wanted her. He had wanted to ruin things for his half-brother. Maybe his motive had been that he couldn't make a go of marriage himself so why should Nigel have the opportunity? Maybe it was revenge for resentments harboured since childhood. The motive didn't really matter. The pattern remained unchanged.

Amy collected the secateurs and other gardening implements. Tom *had* wanted her in one sense. She knew he'd fancied her at first sight—he'd told her as much before he'd kissed her in the summer house. His interest in her had taken a new direction, however, as soon as he'd learned she was about to become engaged to Nigel. Tom hadn't been slow in trying to change her mind, had he? His interest in her and his involvement in her life had escalated from precisely that point. He'd pumped Jennifer for information about her relationship with Nigel. He'd actively discouraged her from trying to sort things out. He'd even offered to marry her himself!

Amy dumped the tools into the box behind the lawnmower and pulled the door of the small wooden shed firmly closed. The thought of Tom's clever campaign made her cringe. He'd been so casual. Throw-away comments like that proposal, the determination to make her laugh and feel better about herself. She'd been so grateful for his subtle expertise in restoring her self-esteem after that incident with Nigel and the contaminated blood samples. He'd supported her on a personal level and he'd praised her on a professional one. Had it been at that point she'd fallen in love with Tom without realising it?

Nigel had played the game, too. His offer of reconciliation had only come after he'd overheard Tom's invitation to go ice skating or something less strenuous. Then Tom had played an ace by deliberately sabotaging the planned date with Nigel, making sure he'd been available to pick up the pieces. The perfect opportunity to bolster her self-esteem again and pull her more

firmly into his camp. The two men had simply been
competing with each other and Amy had been a convenient pawn. Had Tom's wife been another such play-
ing piece?

Amy was staring at the garden without seeing it.
Deliberately, she focused, trying to distract herself yet
again. The owners of the villa had been heavily into a
cottage garden look. Camellias and rhododendrons,
roses and perennials filled the borders. Amy suddenly
disliked the contrived effect immensely. Her passion
was for native plants. Huge evergreen, pittosporum
trees with pale green and cream variegated leaves, off-
set by the rich dark green of coprosma. She loved the
contrast that came with the glossy hand-like leaves of
pseudopanax and the delicate fern-like foliage of the
kowhai. The colours could still be there. Hebes like the
New Zealand lilac with sprays of palest blue flowers.
Dramatic Chatam Island forget-me-nots and pretty
Reinga Reinga lilies. She knew exactly what sort of
garden she would want to create herself. She had seen
it, surrounding that house in Governers Bay.

With that neat turn, Amy's thoughts spiralled back
towards Tom. That had been the cruellest part of his
campaign by far. To let her think that he wanted her
no matter what. To let her dream of a future in which
she could dance. Amy turned her back on the garden.
A soak in a hot tub would fix the pain in her leg.
Tomorrow she would return to work. Maybe immers-
ing herself in her career would do something for the
pain in her soul.

There was plenty of distraction available. The emergency department was inundated. Beds overflowed
from the main front area and the observation ward to

line the corridors. No sooner had one resus area become available than another acute case would arrive
through the ambulance bay doors. The waiting room
was full and the advertised waiting times for non-
urgent cases grew steadily longer.

Patrick Moore, the elderly Irishman, came in but he
wasn't drunk this time. The chest pain he was suffering
was severe enough to warrant monitoring and diagno-
sis. Amy wasn't assigned to Patrick as his nurse but
she took a moment to greet him.

'Ah, Amy.' The old man smiled with difficulty. 'It's
good that you're here. I think I need an angel today.'

'I'm not looking after you today, Patrick,' Amy said
sadly, as she squeezed his hand. 'But I'll come and see
you as soon as I can.' She had to turn away abruptly.
A stretcher was incoming and the ambulance crew
looked serious.

'This is Cathy Hanson,' the ambulance officer told
Amy. 'She collapsed in the supermarket, having experienced sudden onset abdominal pain. She's thirty-
four weeks pregnant.'

Amy was nodding. 'I know Cathy.' She reached for
the patient's hand. Cathy's left arm was still in a heavy
plaster cast. It had only been a couple of weeks since
the surgery on her elbow.

'Amy? Thank God it's you.' Cathy's face was white.
'It's the baby. I think I'm bleeding.' The grip on Amy's
hand was painfully tight. 'It's too early.' Cathy's face
twisted. 'I don't want to lose my baby, Amy,' she
sobbed. 'It's all I have left of Jack.'

Peter came up to Amy. 'I've just cleared Resus 4.
Let's move.'

They moved with speed. Tom appeared as Amy
whisked the curtains shut.

'Call Paediatrics,' Tom instructed Peter. 'And get an incubator down here. Just in case.'

Amy was removing the last of Cathy's clothing. 'You're not bleeding,' she reassured her. 'It's amniotic fluid. Your waters have broken.' Amy looked at Tom. 'There's definite meconium staining in the fluid,' she told him quietly.

'I have to push,' gasped Cathy.

Amy had to step aside as Tom reached between Cathy's legs. 'Get some gloves on,' Tom ordered her. 'And I want the obstetrics trolley. *Now!*'

Consultants Susan Scott and Gareth Harvey joined the team, along with more nurses. The delivery happened so fast that Amy fumbled to try and keep up.

'Cord clamps,' Tom ordered. 'And scissors.'

Amy ripped open a sterile infant blanket pack. Her eyes were glued to the scrap of humanity Tom was holding.

'Get some suction,' Tom said quietly. 'And oxygen.'

Peter held the end of the oxygen tube near the baby's blue face. Tom used a soft tube attached to the suction unit to clear the mouth and nose. Susan was now looking after Cathy, waiting for the delivery of the placenta. Tom and Gareth concentrated on the baby boy, who was still unresponsive.

'One minute Apgar score of 3,' Gareth reported.

'Get a bag mask unit, Amy.'

Amy fitted the miniature mask to the infant ventilator bag. She caught a glimpse of Cathy's terrified face and felt a wash of the same fear. It would be too much to bear if Cathy lost her baby as well as her husband.

The faint mew of sound when Tom lifted the mask clear a minute later made everyone pause in their tasks to watch. The baby cried again, a little more strongly, and Amy could see the skin becoming rapidly pinker. The paediatric team arrived with the incubator and Resus 4 became so crowded that Amy found herself being edged out. It wasn't until they were ready to transfer both Cathy and the baby boy to the obstetric ward and the neonatal intensive care unit that Amy had a chance to say anything more to her patient. She had been avidly following the communication between the specialists.

'He's beautiful, Cathy,' she whispered. 'And he's a good weight. Four pounds is excellent for thirty-four weeks. He probably won't even have to stay in the incubator very long.'

'I know.' Cathy smiled through her tears. 'I feel very lucky.'

'What are you going to call him?'

'Jack. Will you come and see us on the ward?'

'Try and keep me away.' Amy smiled. 'I'll come up as soon as I get my lunch-break.'

Patrick was still being monitored in Resus 6 but Amy was too busy to see him immediately. Another ambulance was backing in to the bay and a man stood near the automatic doors, unable to enter without the security code. He was holding a large bunch of flowers and Amy assumed he was a relative coming in with a patient transfer from another hospital. He came in with the ambulance crew but went straight towards Amy. It still took a moment to recognise him. Patients often looked quite different standing up.

'Stephen,' the man reminded her. 'Stephen Parks. I had my appendix out last week?'

'Of course.' Amy smiled. She looked at the expensive, beautifully cut suit Stephen was wearing. 'I didn't recognise you with clothes on.'

They both smiled. Then Stephen held out the enormous bouquet. 'I just brought these in,' he said offhandedly. 'To say thank you…'

'They're gorgeous.' Amy could see Tom outside cubicle 2. He was staring at the scene. Did he think Stephen Parks was showing an interest in her? Amy bit her lip, wondering how she should deal with this.

'To Janice,' Stephen continued. His smile broadened. 'Is she busy right now?'

'I'll find out.' Amy knew where Janice was at the moment. In cubicle 2. With Tom Barlow.

'There's someone here to see you, Janice. When you have a moment.'

'Is it Stephen?' Having already turned away, Amy didn't see Janice's face brighten. 'He said he might come in today.'

Tom didn't seem to notice Amy. He was watching Janice. 'Don't be long,' he told her. 'I need you in here.'

He was still watching Janice as she moved towards the sorting desk. Amy turned away. What was it Tom had said that night in the pub? It was when things were hard to catch that you knew you really wanted them? She tried not to watch the interchange as Stephen gave Janice the bouquet. She had no intention of checking to see whether Tom was watching. She knew he would be. There was nothing like a bit of competition to clarify the important issues—although Amy was certain that Janice would consider Stephen too old for her. She'd already staked her claim on Tom anyway.

Amy wasn't going to fall to pieces at work. She had plenty to distract herself with, even on her lunch-break. Patrick was being seen by a cardiology registrar so she had to postpone that visit. Instead, she went to the hospital gift shop and purchased a tiny blue teddy bear. Amy was disappointed to find that Cathy was also tied up with an examination in the obstetric ward. She had twenty minutes of her break to fill in so she started walking and went out the side entrance of the block, intending to get some fresh air by the river.

'I thought I might find you here.'

Amy looked up in dismay. She had chosen the same seat that had provided a refuge after Jason Kingsley's death. Had Tom come looking for her or was this an unfortunate coincidence?

'I wanted to talk to you,' Tom said heavily.

'I have to go back.' Amy tried to stand but Tom caught her wrist. 'I don't want to talk to you, Tom.'

'Maybe not. But maybe you owe me the chance to tell you my side of the story. It might be a little different to the impression Nigel left you with.'

'Does it matter what I think?' Amy sat down again and turned her face away from Tom.

'Perhaps it does. What *do* you think, Amy?'

Amy was silent for a long moment. 'I think Nigel was right,' she said eventually, her tone wooden. 'You've used me to try and get back at him. Quite successfully and not for the first time, apparently.'

Tom made an angry noise. 'Listen, Amy. Nigel blamed me for the break-up of his parents' marriage. His father met my mother. They fell in love and she got pregnant—with me. He left Lorraine. And Nigel. Therefore, it was my fault. Never mind the fact that the marriage had been desperately unhappy or the fact that my father tried to keep his relationship with Nigel going despite Lorraine's total obstruction. Thanks to her, he learned to hate his father—and me, until it was convenient for Lorraine to change her mind.'

'What do you mean by that?'

'Lorraine was never out of relationships very long. She married Simon Wesley only six months after my father divorced her and Nigel chose to take his new father's name—hence our different surnames. She and Simon liked to travel and having a child around became an inconvenience for the newly-weds. Boarding school worked well but there were the problems of the holidays.'

'So?'

'So when I was about two or three years old, Nigel started coming to stay with us during school holidays. He hated it. He hated his father and my mother. Most of all he hated me. He was eight years older than me and he made my life a total misery when I was a kid. I dreaded school holidays.'

Amy's sympathies were unexpectedly for Nigel. 'He must have been a very unhappy child.'

Tom gave her a wounded look. 'He wasn't the only one.'

'Didn't your parents help you?'

'They never knew. Nigel learned very early that he could get away with anything if he behaved well when being observed. My mother often wondered why I got so many bruises when Nigel came to stay. They assumed we were just being boys and enjoying a bit of rough and tumble.'

'And you never told?'

'Nigel made it very clear what would happen if I did. I was terrified of him.'

'That's awful.' Amy frowned but her sympathy was too late. Tom shrugged it off.

'He stopped coming when I was about eight. We only saw him occasionally over the next ten years. We shifted to the UK which was where my mother came from. I was about to start medical school when both my parents were killed in a car accident. Our father had been a wealthy man and the inheritance was divided equally between myself and Nigel. Over a million pounds each.'

Amy looked up in surprise. She wouldn't have thought of Tom as a wealthy man. His style and tastes were nothing like those of the Wesleys and their ilk. 'That's a lot of money,' she observed. 'I would have expected Nigel to have been more than happy with his share.'

'So would I,' Tom agreed. 'I thought that was the end of it. I never expected to hear from Nigel again, but he arrived on the doorstep one day. He was doing some overseas travel. I think he wanted to find out whether the will had been totally fair. I got the impression that Lorraine had made spectacular inroads on his own share by that stage. She had been outraged that the inheritance hadn't been divided three ways to include her. Anyway, Nigel had a girlfriend in tow. Nicola, her name was.'

Amy recognised the significance in Tom's face. 'The woman you stole?'

'I didn't encourage her,' Tom said impatiently. 'Unfortunately, she decided I was a better bet than Nigel. She dumped him and started ringing me up.'

'And you ended up marrying her,' Amy finished for him.

Tom laughed. 'I never even dated the girl.' He sobered quickly. 'No. Nigel never met the woman I married. He knows nothing about her.'

'Except that the marriage didn't last very long.' Amy couldn't help the slightly acerbic comment.

'No, it didn't.' Tom's face was very still. 'Do you want to know why it didn't last very long, Amy?'

Amy shifted on the seat uncomfortably. 'Do you want to tell me?'

'Her name was Lucy,' Tom said by way of answer. 'She was quite beautiful. Her mother was part Spanish and Lucy had inherited her black hair but she got her blue eyes from her Irish father.'

'Sounds a bit like Janice.' Amy's hands were gripped together tightly in her lap. And nothing at all like herself.

'I suppose she was.' Tom sounded surprised. 'I hadn't thought of that.' He cleared his throat. 'Lucy was in my class at medical school. We had a bit of a competition going to see which one of us could top the class every year.'

Tom smiled wryly. 'Usually, it was me. The year that Lucy won was when I asked her to marry me. Right there in front of everyone crammed in to see the finals' results. She agreed and there was one hell of a party that night.'

Tom stared ahead of him, clearly unaware of the view. 'We both got jobs at the same hospital after we got married. We even found a flat in London we could afford. We were both too busy to see much of each other, though, and it only lasted for three months before our world fell apart overnight.' Tom dragged his hand over his face. 'Lucy got sick and was diagnosed as having acute myeloid leukaemia.'

'Oh, God!' Amy breathed. A vivid image of Jason Kingsley sprang to mind.

Tom didn't seem to hear her. 'We tried everything,' he continued quietly. 'And then more. I had myself tested as a possible bone-marrow donor. Nothing helped. It was one setback after another. It took nearly a year.'

Amy couldn't look at Tom. The thought that he'd had to physically prevent her from trying to resuscitate Jason when he must have been reliving his own horror was unthinkable. She had thought that his lack of compassion when explaining the situation to her had been caused by his reappraisal of herself. She had even accused him of being unfeeling. It had been unforgivable.

'I'm sorry, Tom.' The words felt hopelessly inadequate. 'I don't know what to say.'

'You don't need to say anything,' Tom assured her. 'I must admit that having Jason Kingsley as a patient, however briefly, brought the past back a little too closely for comfort, but in a way it was—' His words were cut off by the strident beeping of his pager. It wasn't the normal call sign.

'There's a cardiac arrest in Emergency.' Tom stated what Amy already knew. 'Let's go.'

They both ran. They were both too late to be of any use. Patrick Moore had died while they sat by the river. Amy was stunned by her unexpected sense of loss. Subdued, she helped Peter tidy up the resus area and prepare Patrick for his last exit from Emergency. There would never be anyone with a lilting Irish accent calling her an angel again. There would probably never be anyone calling her that at all. Not Patrick. And not Tom. It didn't matter. It had been a silly nickname anyway. Too corny for words. Only it hadn't sounded silly when Tom had used it.

Amy found the rest of her shift dragged. She wanted some time to herself to digest what Tom had told her. The information had certainly undermined the shock she'd been in since hearing of his marriage from Nigel.

Could it change anything else? Amy didn't want to talk
to Tom again until she'd had time to think so she
avoided contact for the rest of the afternoon.

She didn't have to avoid Tom the next day as he
was rostered off. Janice began her morning teabreak
complaining that she wasn't rostered off. It was far too
nice a day to be stuck at work.

'Never mind,' Janice decided. 'I've got four days
off, starting tomorrow, and I'm going to make the most
of it. I might even have some news when I get back.'

'Where are you going?' Jennifer asked.

'Just away.'

'Who with?'

'Not telling.' Janice smiled secretly. 'I'm not one to
tempt fate. You'll see when I get back.' She extended
the fingers of her left hand and gave them a contem-
plative glance. There could be no mistaking the hint.

Tom was still absent the following day. So was
Janice. Amy was beginning to feel that the world she
had known was simply evaporating around her.
Jennifer hadn't returned home last night. She hadn't
even come back for a clean uniform that morning so
the overnight stay had been more premeditated than
previously. When she arrived at work, Jennifer was ra-
diating happiness. Amy just smiled and kept going towards the sluice room. She wasn't sure she was the
best person to talk to Jennifer right now. She didn't
want to dampen her friend's pleasure in life.

Jennifer appeared in the sluice room less than a minute later.

'*There* you are, Amy! Guess what?'

'What?' Amy looked at the contents of the suction
container with distaste as she eased the lid off.

'It's Noel's birthday next week.'

'That's great.' Amy emptied the container and flushed away the remnants as she rinsed it.

'We're going to have a party on Saturday to celebrate. We're going shopping tonight for wine and food. Do you want to come and help push the trolley?'

'I think you'll manage without me.' Amy unclipped the disposable tubing and folded it into the contaminated waste container.

'I feel bad that you're spending so much time by yourself.' Jennifer chewed her bottom lip. 'I'm not much of a flatmate at the moment, am I?'

'You've got more important things happening.' Amy smiled at her friend. 'It's OK. I understand and I'm really pleased you're happy.'

'I've never been so happy,' Jennifer confessed. 'I think Noel's going to ask me to marry him. Maybe it'll happen at the party.'

'You never know. All sorts of things can happen at parties.' Amy reached for the Presept tablets. She dropped them into the container of water to make up the sterilising solution for the suction kit. Her smile was wry. 'Look at what happened at the last party I went to.'

'You'll still come to this one, won't you?' Jennifer asked anxiously.

'Depends who else is coming,' Amy said evasively.

'We won't be inviting Nigel.' Jennifer grinned. 'Consultants are off the list. Except for Tom, of course, but he might not get back in time.'

'Back?' Amy stripped off her gloves. 'Back from where?'

'Auckland. He decided at the last minute to attend an emergency medicine conference.'

'And he got leave? Just like that?'

'Mmm.' Jennifer shrugged. 'If you ask me, Gareth is bending over backwards to be accommodating. He really wants Tom to take on the consultancy here permanently. From what I hear, the job's his if he wants it.'

'Why wouldn't he?' Amy led the way out of the sluice room.

'Well...' Jennifer hesitated. 'I'm not supposed to know this but Noel told me they've offered Tom his old job back in Chicago. That's why he's gone to Auckland.'

'I don't follow you.'

'One of the invited speakers is the head of the trauma team in Tom's old hospital. He's dead keen to have Tom back and persuaded him to attend the conference so they could discuss it.'

Amy said nothing. She was too stunned trying to contemplate a complete exit by Tom Barlow from her life. The prospect wasn't welcome. And where had Janice gone on her time off? Just away? Where to? *Auckland?*

'Apparently they've made an incredible offer. Noel thinks he'd be mad to turn it down. He said he'd jump at the chance.'

Amy followed the direction of Jennifer's gaze and spotted Noel in the emergency department, heading for one of the cubicles.

'Oh, good,' Jennifer murmured. 'I think that's one of my patients. I'll catch you later, Amy.'

'What would you do if Noel did take a job overseas?' Amy asked curiously.

'Go with him, of course.' Jennifer's grin was cheeky. 'He's not getting rid of me that easily.'

Amy watched Jennifer disappear behind the curtain

of cubicle 3. Was that an incentive for Tom to leave
the country? To get rid of complications in his life?
Like her?

The rest of the week passed painfully slowly. Any satisfaction with work was muted. Amy only saw Jennifer
during the hours that their shifts coincided and the
party was the consuming topic of interest for her friend.
Amy worked an early shift on Saturday, finishing at
3 p.m. There was no escaping having to attend the
party that night.

'I came to yours, didn't I?' Jennifer had played her
ace the day before. 'I didn't want to but it turned out
to be the best thing I ever did. Remember when I said
I thought it might be the turning point of my life? I
was right, wasn't I? That was when it all started with
Noel. You have to come to our party, Amy.'

'I suppose so,' Amy had agreed reluctantly. 'Seeing
as you came to mine under duress.'

'Who knows?' Jennifer had suggested happily.
'Maybe *this* one will be the turning point of *your* life.'

At least Amy wouldn't make quite the fashion statement Jennifer had achieved at the Wesleys'. She had
nothing suitable to wear so she used the few hours
before the party to go shopping. The black silky trousers she found were perfect. Wide enough to disguise
her legs completely. She chose a matching black top
that would be elegant enough for any special occasion.
Buttons ran down the front from a scooped neckline
and the soft fabric hung in folds from a high yoke. As
she dressed later, Amy added a long chain of tiny gold
hearts that had belonged to her mother. She brushed
her hair out and wore it loose, keeping stray curls in
place with a black velvet headband. Amy took more

care than usual with her make-up, using foundation to
cover the dark circles that had appeared under her eyes
that week. She didn't want to have to ward off any
solicitous comments regarding her health or well-being.

The party was being held at Noel's parents' house.
A large crowd had gathered and the atmosphere was
lively. Jennifer spotted Amy's arrival and dragged her
off to the kitchen to meet Noel's mother, Maggie. Then
she steered her to where Noel's father was pouring
drinks.

'Aren't they great?' Jennifer whispered to Amy as
they moved away. 'I think his mother actually likes
me.'

'Of course she does.' Amy smiled. Noel's mother
had improbably bright red hair and could have been
competing with Jennifer for the amount of jewellery
that could be worn on a single occasion. Obviously
kindred spirits.

'I had to check her out,' Jennifer said with a grin,
'in case she was a vampire.'

Amy didn't need any reminders of her last party. She
eyed her glass of sparkling wine and wondered if juice
might have been a wiser choice.

'I'll be back soon,' Jennifer told Amy. 'I'm just going to help Maggie with those salads in the kitchen.'

'I'll come and help, too,' Amy offered.

'No—absolutely not! You're here to enjoy yourself.'
Jennifer gave her a friendly push towards the terrace.
'Go and circulate. There's a very nice man setting up
the barbecue. He's Noel's cousin. If you haven't said
hello by the time I get back, I'll introduce you.'

Amy obediently headed for the terrace where the
party group was congregating, attracted by the aroma
of a cooking process already under way. She avoided

the knot of people, presumably including Noel's cousin, who were discussing the marinating of a spit roast. She took a moment to admire the terrace, which was lit by strings of fairy lights. French doors opened to the house and the music volume was increasing. A few couples began to dance on the flagged terrace.

Amy edged her way to a small garden bench, partly screened by shrubs, to watch the scene. New arrivals were coming out through the French doors to join the group on the terrace. The dancing couples were between Amy and the house so her view was patchy, as though lit by a very slow strobe light. There was no mistaking what she saw, however.

Janice was looking breathtaking in a white trouser suit. Her laughter and smiles made everyone turn, and nobody could miss the large cluster of diamonds prominent on her left hand. What made Amy's heart lurch painfully was that her right hand was linked firmly into the arm of her partner. And the man beside her was Tom Barlow.

Amy stared.

As though he could feel her gaze, Tom looked straight towards where she was sitting. She saw him excuse himself from the group of well wishers that had gathered and he moved through the dancers with graceful ease.

Amy knew she should offer some congratulations but the lump in her throat made speech impossible. It was Tom who spoke first, having sat beside her in silence for what seemed a long time.

'Are you all right, Amy? It feels like I haven't seen you for ages.'

'I'm fine,' Amy managed after another short silence. 'How was the conference?'

'Interesting.' Tom was looking at Amy but she didn't quite meet his gaze. 'It was good to have a few days away. I needed the space to think about a few things.' He paused. 'I needed to make a few decisions. I think it helped, having a bit of distance.'

Amy nodded. It was clear that one large decision had been made.

'I've bought the house, Amy.' Tom sounded excited. 'You know, the one in Governers Bay?'

'I know.' The thought of Janice sharing that house with Tom made Amy feel sick. She closed her eyes for a second. 'It's a lovely house,' she said faintly.

'Yes, it is, isn't it?'

The polite and meaningless exchange struck Amy as absurd. The whole setting seemed incongruous with its lights and laughter and music. Amy could see Janice moving through the groups of people on the terrace, displaying her engagement ring with blatant triumph.

'I'm thinking of moving, myself,' she told Tom calmly.

'Really?'

'Jen's not around much now. At the rate she and Noel are going, I'll be on my own all the time soon. It's time to move on, I think.'

'To a new flat?'

'Maybe a new job.'

Tom leaned closer. 'Sorry, I can't hear you very well, Amy. This music is a bit loud.'

Amy could see Noel coming towards them, carrying a bottle of champagne in one hand, glasses in the other. Jennifer was beside him, grinning from ear to ear. Maybe they were about to announce their own happy event. Jen would be able to compare rings with Janice. Maybe even arrange a double wedding. Amy stood up hurriedly. She didn't want to know. Not right now.

'Tom—congratulations! I just heard!' Noel waved the bottle of champagne. 'Time for some heavy celebration.'

Tom stood up to receive a congratulatory hug from Jennifer. 'I'm so pleased for you, Tom,' Jennifer said excitedly.

Amy edged backwards, then she turned and quietly made her way through the gathering and into the house. She had to leave. She might have to accept the decisions other people were making about their lives, but she couldn't pretend to share their joy. It was definitely time to leave.

In more ways than one.

CHAPTER NINE

'YOU can't mean it, Amy.'

Amy stared at the pile of journals on Gareth Harvey's desk. As the medical director of the emergency department, it was only courtesy that demanded Amy inform him of her intention to resign.

'Did you know that Angela is taking up a position in CCU?'

Amy nodded. Angela Parkinson had been a nurse manager in the department for longer than Amy had been there. She had been voicing her desire for a change from emergency medicine for some time now.

'We're going to have to fill the nurse manager position here,' Gareth pointed out. 'You're the obvious choice, Amy.'

'I am?' Amy was startled out of her silence. She hadn't considered that possibility.

'Of course you are. You're one of the best nurses we've ever had in the department. I had hoped that your skill and dedication to the job meant that this was an area you were happy to stay in.'

'I'm not planning to leave nursing,' Amy said quickly. 'Or even emergency work. I just feel like I need a new direction. A fresh start somewhere else.'

'A fresh start might not be in a position that carries this much responsibility. It might well not be in your best interests if you want to move your career forward. Wouldn't such a big step-up provide enough of a new direction? It's quite a challenge,' Gareth continued persuasively. 'It's an opportunity a lot of people would jump at.'

'I know,' Amy acknowledged. She would have jumped at it herself a month or two ago. The decision to leave had not come easily, however. She couldn't afford to relinquish the potential solution to her problems.

Gareth shook his head. 'But you'd still like me to write you a reference for another job.'

'Yes, please.'

'You'll need to make your resignation official. There will be a few weeks' notice to work through.' He gave Amy a concerned look. 'Do me a favour, Amy?'

'What's that?'

'Think about it a little longer. If I don't receive anything official on my desk I'll forget we had this conversation. If I do, I'll have a reference ready for you.' Gareth smiled. 'And it will be an excellent one.'

'Thanks.' Amy smiled her agreement at the imposed condition. If it made Gareth happy she would wait a few days, but her mind was made up. He wasn't going to talk her out of what seemed like a brave new beginning for herself.

The first step taken, Amy left the director's office with a lighter step. Laura called out as she passed the sorting desk.

'The new rosters are out, Amy.' She handed over a sheet of paper. 'You've got four night shifts next week.'

'I don't mind,' Amy said truthfully, having scanned the consultant names for the shifts. The less she saw of Tom in the next few weeks, the better. Leaving would be less painful that way.

Awareness of Tom's presence in the department was

a constant disturbance. She could avoid direct conversation unless she was working with him. She could
avoid direct eye contact almost all the time, but there
was no way of avoiding the awareness her body had
of his presence. It had, after all, been the first thing
she'd noticed about this man. The way the sound of
his laughter had struck a sensitive chord. The way his
eye contact had left a physical impression of being
touched. It had been disturbing right from the start.
Maybe her body had fallen in love with Tom all by
itself. It had just taken longer for her mind and soul to
catch up.

Amy avoided the staffroom completely. She couldn't
cope with the endless round of similar conversations as
more staff members noticed the engagement ring on
show. Not Janice's spectacular ring. This one belonged
to Jennifer. As she'd suspected, Noel had ended the
celebration of his birthday by proposing to Jennifer.

'My ring's not nearly as flashy as Janice's,' Jennifer
had confessed to Amy happily two days ago. 'But I
love it.'

Janice, thankfully, was nowhere to be seen. The
younger nurse wasn't bothered by any requirements to
work out her notice.

'She's never going to work again,' Jennifer had relayed to Amy the previous. 'You have to hand it to
her, I guess. She said she'd get married by the time
she was twenty-five and she goes and lands a million-
aire to boot. Who would have believed it?'

Amy would. She didn't share her friend's amaze-
ment at the unexpected bonus Janice had gained. Amy
already knew about the inheritance Tom had received
from his father. She avoided the subject as much as
possible, even with Jennifer. Her campaign to convince

her friend that she had no romantic interest in Tom had been more successful than intended. It had hurt that Jen had been as happy as everyone else to offer her congratulations to Tom on the night of the party. Her campaign to hide her present distress and not dampen Jennifer's joy was also an obvious success. Jen's smile now, as she emerged from a cubicle, was as brilliant as ever.

'Is that the new roster?' Jennifer peered over Amy's shoulder. 'Thank God for that—no nights.' She kept scanning the sheet. 'You've got four, you poor thing!'

'I don't mind. I quite like working nights.'

'I won't see you.'

'You don't much anyway, these days.' Amy delivered the observation with an understanding smile. She wasn't complaining.

'I need to talk to you about that, Amy. About the flat.'

'You're going to move in with Noel?'

Jennifer nodded. 'We've set a date for the wedding. It's in January. Will you be my bridesmaid, Amy? Please?'

'Sure.' If she was still in the country. Amy didn't want to upset Jen by casting doubts on her availability. She might still be within easy travelling distance in any case. 'And don't worry about the flat. It's time I moved. I'm sick of looking after that enormous garden. I'll hand in a month's notice on the lease.'

'I'll pay my share of the rent until then.' Jennifer looked at the roster again. 'Do you really not mind working all those nights?'

'It makes a change.' Amy grinned. 'As good as a holiday, so they say.'

* * *

'They' hadn't spent many nights in an emergency department. Certainly, the number of admissions was well
down but it was far from a holiday. People that came
into the emergency department in the small hours were
usually sick enough to need a lot of attention. Staff
numbers were drastically reduced as well so the work-
load was often as demanding as daytime duties. Amy's
nights started at 10 p.m., before the last of the staggered day shifts ended. She finished at 7 a.m., would
be in bed by 8 a.m. and could sleep until late afternoon,
ready for the next night shift. On her fourth night, Amy
went into work earlier than necessary.

Following a now familiar route, Amy made her way
to the neonatal intensive care unit. She stopped short
just outside the window on this occasion, however.
Little Jack Hanson's incubator was empty. The little
blue teddy bear that had been sitting on top of the
incubator for the last ten days was also gone. A nurse
spotted Amy's bewildered gaze.

'Try the paediatric ward.' She smiled. 'He's just having a day or two in there before they let him go home.'

Amy found Cathy and Jack in a private room in the
ward. A normal hospital bassinet stood beside the single bed but it was also empty. The baby lay in his
mother's arms. Or rather, arm. Cathy was becoming
adept at handling her son, despite the unwieldy plaster
cast protecting her left elbow. The two women smiled
at each other. Amy had become a frequent visitor since
Jack's birth and they had become firm friends.

'Would you like to hold him?' Cathy invited.
'Look—no tubes or wires. He doesn't even need the
apnoea monitor any longer.'

Amy was delighted to accept the tiny bundle. She

settled herself on the bed beside Cathy. 'How's it been, being away from the unit?'

'A bit scary at first,' Cathy admitted. 'But now it's wonderful to have some time just to ourselves. There's plenty of help available if I need it but I can shut the door and have Jack all to myself when I want to.'

'And you'll be going home soon?'

'They want me to have some help available so I'll wait until my mum arrives. It's just in case I have problems with my arm, which is fair enough.'

'Have you had that check-up on your elbow?'

'I had X-rays today. It's doing well. The surgeon even came in to see me himself.'

'That must be the new surgeon,' Amy observed. 'Did he have an English accent?'

'No. It was the same man that saw me in Emergency after the accident. The one that did the operation.'

'Nigel Wesley?' Amy was surprised. She thought Nigel had already left for Sydney.

'He said I'd be seeing someone new on my next appointment, because he's leaving.' Cathy smiled. 'I didn't like him much when I first met him but he was very nice to me tonight.'

'He can be nice,' Amy agreed. She frowned. 'You saw him tonight?'

'Just a few minutes before you arrived,' Cathy confirmed. 'They work long hours, these doctors, don't they? Are you still on nights?'

Amy nodded. 'Last one tonight for a while. I'd better go and get on with it, in fact.' She dropped a gentle kiss on the sleeping baby's downy head. 'Shall I put Jack in his bassinet for you?'

'No. I'll hold him again for a while. He's due to get

hungry again any time now. I want to see if I can change his nappy by myself when he wakes up.'

'You'll manage.' Amy carefully transferred the bundle.

'I will, too.' Cathy grinned at Amy. 'Thank heavens for disposables.'

Amy paused when she reached the stairwell. She needed to go downstairs to get to Emergency but directly above her was the floor that contained surgical wards and offices. The knowledge that Nigel was in the building prompted a change in her intended direction. This would probably be her last chance to ever see Nigel, and Amy felt she owed him something. Tom hadn't really said that much about his childhood but there had been a point when Amy had felt sympathy for his half-brother. She had recognised the pain a child felt by rejection—for whatever reason. The guilt had embedded itself a little more firmly since. Amy had known it had been no great love affair between herself and Nigel, but she'd been prepared to use him to gain the home and family which might have made up for the romantic compromise. Then she'd rejected him herself. Very publicly. Had anyone ever genuinely loved Nigel?

Amy found Nigel sitting in his office. The room was completely devoid of personal items. A briefcase lay open on the desk and Nigel was packing the contents of a drawer into it. He put down the stack of personalised stationery when he responded to Amy's tentative knock.

'Come in, Amy.' Nigel scooped a handful of pens from the drawer. 'I'm just getting this office ready for its new owner.' He smiled a shade wistfully. 'Have you come to say goodbye?'

Amy nodded. The things she would have liked to have say were tied up in knots in her head. Nigel watched her hesitation. He put the pens into the brief-case and then stopped his task, leaning his elbows on the desk. His smile was kind. The sort of smile that Amy had seen before—the one that had made her dis-believe that Nigel was as bad as Jennifer and others had made out.

'Did you want to talk to me, Amy?'

'I don't really know what to say,' Amy confessed. 'Except that I'm sorry about the way things have worked out.'

'So am I.' Nigel appeared to be collecting his own thoughts. 'I think we might have been able to make it work, you know, Amy. I knew you didn't really love me but I'm also quite aware that I'm not capable of inspiring that sort of emotion.'

Amy looked down at her feet. Nigel was more astute than she'd given him credit for.

'That kind of devotion only exists for others,' Nigel continued calmly. 'The people who are prepared to take risks. I still wanted what those people seemed to have. Marriage, children. A real family.'

The acknowledgment of an unhappy childhood was unspoken, but the depth of what had been missing from Nigel's life touched Amy.

'I'm sure you'll still find it, Nigel.'

'I doubt that. But if I don't, I won't blame others for it any more. And I won't resent their happiness. Even Tom. He always had what I thought was rightfully mine.'

'It wasn't his fault.'

Nigel nodded a brief agreement. 'The thought that he'd taken your affections was the last straw, really. It blew the top off a rather large can of worms. We had a major row after you left us in the car park that evening. It cleared away quite a few long-standing resentments. We even achieved a kind of peace, I think. We'll never be friends but at least I think we can stop being enemies.'

'Tom's had his own share of knocks.'

'Yes. I hadn't realised. Some people can cope better than others. They don't let the knocks destroy them. They're still prepared to take risks. I'm not.'

'You might be. If you meet the right person, then the risks are worth taking. Maybe you'll find someone in Sydney.'

'Possibly. Who knows?' Nigel shrugged. He wasn't expecting a miracle.

Was Amy? She was planning to follow the same route. To run away and start again somewhere else.

Nigel was smiling at her again. 'You'll make it, Amy. You have the capability to take a situation that's second best and make something good out of it. That's what really attracted me to you.'

'I don't think you know me that well, Nigel.'

'Don't you? I admit it hasn't been long and I knew I was trying to rush you into marriage, but it was quite long enough for me to recognise the strength you have.' The sound Nigel made was almost wistful. 'Probably because I never had it myself. You've had your share of knocks, too, Amy. Your relationship with your parents wasn't much better than mine. You had a disability to cope with on top of that.'

'It's not much of a disability,' Amy said dismissively. 'It's never stopped me doing something I really wanted to do.' She could even dance if she wanted to, Amy decided silently.

'Exactly,' Nigel stated. 'You have an attitude that accepts what can't be changed but you don't let it stop you getting what you want out of life.'

'I don't know about that,' Amy muttered. She'd let it stop her making love with Tom, and she'd wanted that more than anything in her life. She hadn't been prepared to take that risk. If she had, maybe Tom wouldn't have gone looking elsewhere quite so fast. And was she accepting what couldn't be changed now? No. She was planning to run away.

'You're a brilliant nurse, Amy. I've always had the greatest admiration for your capabilities.'

'Thanks.' Amy wanted to return the compliment. 'Your new position in Sydney is a real honour. You deserve it, Nigel.'

'At least I have one area for success in life,' Nigel agreed. 'A career isn't a bad focus, I guess.'

'No.' It was all Amy really had left herself. 'It's not.'

'I won't see you again. I'm leaving very early to-morrow.' Nigel fiddled with the clasp on his briefcase. 'When you see Tom, could you say goodbye on my behalf?'

'Sure.' It was time to leave. 'Good luck, Nigel.'

'And to you, Amy.'

Amy only had five minutes left in which to report for duty. She took the lift. Trying to hurry downstairs was a recipe for disaster in her case. She knew her limits. Did she really know her strengths? It she did, in fact, have the kind of strength Nigel thought she had, maybe she wouldn't need the luck he had offered.

Nigel's observation was surprising to say the least. Was she really able to take a situation that was second best and make something good out of it? Nigel didn't

know she'd run away from her own childhood. She
hadn't even seen her father since the day her mother
had been buried. She'd run from her first serious relationship as well, taking a job in a new city to combat
the rejection that had followed in the wake of her boyfriend's aversion to her scars. Amy had fled any sub-
sequent relationships before they'd even reached that
point. Now she was about to repeat history.

What if she could accept something that couldn't be
changed and make the best of it? She could make that
best something to be really proud of. Amy marched
down the empty corridor, past the closed gift shop and
post office. She could apply for that nurse manager
position and most likely win it, if Gareth was to be
believed. The promotion would mean she could afford
a mortgage on her own house—and garden. Amy hurried past the main entrance now patrolled by security
guards. She could even take dancing lessons.

That clinched it. She was going to meet this challenge. She was never going to run from a difficult situation again. The decision was the right one, she knew
that as soon as she'd made it. The surge of energy that
came with the knowledge was welcome. So was the
satisfaction in defining a direction and goal for herself.
She could build that damned bridge now and she would
be getting over more than her relationship with Nigel
Wesley. Tom Barlow and all the 'what ifs' could join
the other trolls under it.

Tom was finishing his shift as Amy arrived in
Emergency. For a man who'd recently defined his own
new goals he didn't look as happy as Amy now felt.

'Cheer up, Tom. Isn't it time you were heading
home?'

'Are you trying to get rid of me, Amy?' The smile didn't match the watchful expression.

Amy looked away quickly. What if he guessed she had just relegated him to troll country? 'You look a bit tired.'

'I am. I haven't been sleeping too well just lately.'

Amy looked around. Surely there was an urgent task that needed attending to? She didn't want to think about what was keeping Tom from getting enough rest at nights. Why couldn't somebody throw up or something?

'I've been asleep all day,' she said lightly.

'It's obviously agreed with you.'

'I've just been to visit Cathy Hanson. She and baby Jack are doing really well. They're talking about letting her take him home in a few days.'

'How will she manage with a baby? She'll have that cast on her arm for weeks.'

'Her parents are coming to help. She'll manage.' Amy paused. 'I saw Nigel, too. He's leaving for Sydney tomorrow. He said to say goodbye.'

'You saw Nigel?' He frowned as Amy nodded. 'It doesn't look as though he said anything to upset you.'

'No. Quite the contrary.' Amy glimpsed the interpretation Tom was making and laughed. 'It wasn't anything like that, Tom. It's over. It wasn't really there in the first place but it's nice to know that we can both recognise and accept that.'

'It's really over?'

'Yes.' Amy didn't want to discuss it any further. She wanted to move on, not dwell on the past. 'Excuse me, Tom. I need to find something in Gareth's office.' Amy wanted an application form for the nurse manager's

position. 'Get some sleep, Tom,' she advised. 'It'll
make you feel a lot better.'

Amy only had a few hours' sleep herself the following
morning. She wanted to get back into a normal pattern
and sleep that night. The best way to ensure that would
be to get some exercise in the afternoon. The garden
didn't need any attention but a good long walk would
do, so Amy headed for the Port Hills. New inspiration
struck when she reached the top of the Summit Road.
She had seen the sign beside the coffee-shop before but
had never considered taking advantage of the shop's
sideline business of hiring out mountain bikes.

Amy pulled into the car park. Why not? She had
ridden bikes confidently up until her accident. It wasn't
something you forgot how to do entirely. It would be
easier than dancing and she could find out in private
just how far she could push her physical limits. After
a short lesson on the intricacies of the gears and advice
on available tracks, Amy strapped her helmet into position and set off.

It was a long haul up the road winding along the top
of the hill and Amy was gratified to discover she
wasn't as unfit as she'd feared. The bike handled easily
on the relatively smooth surface of the main track but
Amy wasn't content to end the experiment there.
Checking her map as she neared the end of the road,
she chose a smaller loop track around the side of the
hill, designated as medium to difficult. Having made
that decision, she then propped the bike against a fence
and sat on the post for a minute to enjoy the view of
the harbour and hills. Taking a drink from the water
bottle that clipped onto the bike frame, she gazed long
and hard at Quail Island and then searched the shore-

line on her side of the harbour coast, trying to see the green house in its forest. Tom was probably there right now. Maybe Janice was there as well. Amy jumped carefully off the fence post and snapped the water bottle back into place. There was no profit to be gained from following that line of thinking.

She began her negotiation of the new track cautiously, even getting off to push the bike over some of the rougher and steeper segments. Her confidence grew, however, and after an hour, well away from any roads or spectators, Amy found she was having great fun keeping her balance and speed over the rough terrain. The track was getting closer to the harbour as it descended and it felt wonderfully isolated. Apart from some startled sheep and a few fishing boats on the harbour, there was no sign of life. It was surprising there were no other mountain bikers but maybe Amy had chosen one of the less popular routes.

Although her confidence had increased markedly, Amy paused at the top of the steepest decline she had so far encountered. The bend it took further on wasn't too sharp but Amy didn't want a spill to mar her first outing so she decided to get off and push the bike again. Amy had no inkling that she wasn't alone until she heard the warning shout behind her. Another cyclist had come over the top of the sharp drop at considerable speed. Amy barely had time to turn her head before the collision occurred. Tangled in her bike, Amy hurtled off the side of the bend she had been trying to avoid. She was dimly aware of the rocks and scrubby branches dotting the hillside she was rolling down. The solid rock that finally broke the fall as the ground levelled out crushed the bicycle frame against her leg.

Amy felt the bone in her thigh snap with a sickening crunch.

The pain came a few seconds later and Amy almost lost consciousness from its first assault.

'Are you all right?' The other cyclist had scrambled down the hillside. 'God, I'm so sorry—there was just no way I could stop.'

'Not your fault,' Amy gasped. 'I should have been watching.'

The young man looked at the bicycle over Amy's legs. 'You're bleeding,' he observed nervously. He peered more closely. 'God, your leg's a bit of a mess.'

Amy struggled to prop herself up on one elbow. 'See if you can lift the bicycle without moving my leg,' she requested. 'I'm pretty sure it's broken.'

'The bicycle certainly is.' The stranger gave Amy a very wry grin as he carefully pulled the mangled machine clear. Amy tried to smile back but there was enough movement to bring on a fresh wave of agony. She cried out and was forced to lie down again.

'Oh, God.' The young man looked as agonised as Amy felt. 'My name's Shane,' he told Amy. 'I don't know anything much about first aid but shouldn't I see if you've got a pulse or something?'

Amy almost laughed. 'I'm still alive, Shane. I think it's just my leg I've injured, but I'm going to need some help.'

'I'll go.' Shane got hurriedly to his feet.

'Hang on.' Amy was panting. Was it the pain or did she have other injuries that might be causing her shortness of breath? She turned her neck cautiously and tilted her chin towards her chest. No pain. She wiggled her fingers and the toes on her right foot. Nothing felt too strange so maybe she didn't need to worry about a spinal injury. She felt her abdomen as best she could. Nothing hurt too badly. Amy took a deep breath and decided she didn't have any broken ribs. She was probably fairly bruised but she was confident that the only major problem was her leg. The knowledge wasn't enough to allay the fear Amy was experiencing, however. If the blood loss was serious enough then she would be threatened by hypovolaemic shock. That was a condition that could easily prove fatal if not treated quickly enough. 'How badly is my leg bleeding?' she asked Shane anxiously.

'It's a bit messy,' Shane concluded after another cautious look. 'Your jeans are pretty soaked but it's not gushing or anything. There's a nasty chopped-up bit on top with some white stuff in the middle.'

'That's my bone.' Amy tried to catch her breath and fought a rising tide of nausea. Shane's inexpert appraisal was consistent with a nasty compound fracture. She would be losing blood internally even if he couldn't see anything dramatic from the outside. 'Listen, Shane, have you got something clean you could cover the chopped-up bit with?'

'Only my T-shirt.' Shane looked dubious.

'That's better than nothing. There's a good chance of getting an infection in an open fracture if it's not covered quickly.' Amy closed her eyes. The effort to talk was becoming greater.

'You sound like you know what you're talking about.'

'I do. I'm an emergency department nurse.' Amy opened her eyes. 'My name is Amy Brooks,' she told Shane. 'Please, go for help and tell them...' Amy could feel a new threat, that of fainting. 'Tell them it's urgent.'

'I will. God, I'll go as fast as I can.' Shane folded his T-shirt and laid the cleanest part gently over Amy's injury. He looked as pale as Amy suspected she was looking herself. 'This is all my fault,' he berated himself, beginning a mad scramble back up the hillside.

Seconds later, Amy was astonished to see Shane, naked from the waist up, on his bike, heading down the hillside she was lying on. She managed to raise herself on one elbow again briefly. Long enough to see him reach the fence at the far end of the sheep paddock, lift his bike over and leap over the fence himself, cycling even faster as the ground flattened out before disappearing from sight down another slope. A minute later, she could hear distant shouting. It was even more of a struggle to raise her head this time. All she could see were the fishing boats. One was moving towards the shore but it was probably only coincidence.

Amy's teeth were chattering and her head bumped against the ground as she tried to lower herself down again. Waves of pain, nausea and dizziness combined to drive any grip on reality further away. It was impossible to judge how much time was passing. Or whether any help would even arrive. She was oblivious to the sound of the approaching helicopter and to the sight of panicked sheep trying to escape the flat portion of their paddock as the helicopter landed. Amy did become aware of a new sensation of pain, however, as something was rubbed hard on her collarbone. Then she became aware of the voices.

'Responsive to painful stimuli,' someone said.

'Open your eyes, Amy,' someone else ordered. She knew that voice. Amy tried, but she couldn't get her eyes to co-operate. She tried to say something but only a groan escaped her lips. She gave up and listened to the voices instead.

'I'd put her GCS at less than 9.'

'What's the pulse like?'

'Tachycardia of 130. Low volume.'

'I'm not surprised. She's lost a lot of blood from this fracture.'

'Hare traction splint?'

'Let's get an IV in first. What about the BP?'

'Ninety systolic.'

'Let's get two IV lines in, then.'

Amy felt the prick of the needles in her arms. The voices continued and Amy made a huge effort to open her eyes.

'Tom!' It came out as only a whisper, but he heard it. His face loomed closer. 'What are you…doing here?'

'I was talking to one of the paramedics when the call came through.' Tom was touching her face. 'I persuaded them to let me tag along. You had me worried sick, Amy Brooks.'

Someone was touching Amy's leg. Cutting away the remnants of her jeans. Amy cried out in pain.

'Give her some morphine,' someone directed. 'Draw up 10 mg and give her 5 now.'

Tom's hand was on Amy's forehead. 'You're going to be all right, Amy. You've broken your leg. We're going to splint it as soon as you've got some morphine on board.' He stroked her hair. She hadn't been aware of her crash helmet being removed. 'What were you trying to do, angel?'

'I wanted…' Amy could feel the effects of the morphine kicking in. Her voice trailed away to an inaudible whisper.

'I wanted…to dance.'

CHAPTER TEN

EVERYBODY could see Amy's leg now.

The external fixation of the fracture made her leg look like something caged in a zoo. Judging by the number of people coming in to peer at it, it was a major attraction.

And Amy didn't mind a bit.

The orthopaedic team's ward round began early. Amy, still drowsy from the general anaesthetic and the post-surgical analgesia, was bemused by the number of medical personnel gathered around her bed and the almost party atmosphere of introductions and small talk. Noel was closest to the head of Amy's bed. She caught his eye.

'What's all this about?'

'You created a bit of stir.' Noel grinned. 'Our new surgeon, Martin Southerby, was having a tour of the place when you were brought in. Your leg was such a mess that Martin got pretty excited. The team that was actually on call persuaded him to scrub in and he ended up doing your surgery himself.' Noel tutted with mock disapproval. 'We were in Theatre for nearly three hours. If it hadn't been you, Jen would have been rather annoyed at missing our date.'

The new surgeon, a tall man in his late forties, had finished shaking hands with the collection of nursing staff from the ward. He turned his attention to Amy.

'You're my first patient in this country,' he informed

her. 'You'd better make a spectacular recovery, young lady, or my reputation will be ruined.'

'I'll do my best,' Amy promised. The surgeon had a very intelligent face and a lovely smile. She liked him.

'How much do you know about your injury?' Martin asked.

'Nothing at all,' Amy responded. 'I've just woken up properly.'

'How are you feeling?'

'Surprisingly good.' Amy smiled again. 'My leg's not hurting much at all.'

'Good.' Martin Southerby's expression became serious. 'You had a rather nasty compound fracture there, Amy. Comminuted, with extensive soft-tissue damage.'

Amy nodded. A comminuted fracture meant that the bone had fragmented into more than two pieces. It could be a serious injury.

'We also had to cope with a lot of old scar tissue,' Martin continued. 'I understand you had a childhood injury of some severity.'

Amy nodded again. 'Was that a problem?'

'It was certainly a challenge.' The surgeon smiled. 'I got the impression that your original injury hadn't been well managed. Getting a true alignment was difficult and we needed a bit of extra bone to fill in the gaps. You'll notice a sore patch on one hip later. We borrowed a plug or two of bone from there.'

'So my leg will be straighter than it was?' Amy's eyes widened.

'Absolutely. I made sure I got them the same length.' The surgeon looked at Amy quizzically. 'You must have been having difficulty with that leg for years. Did you not ever think of having it corrected?'

'I learned to cope,' Amy said simply. 'I preferred to ignore it.'

'You might find this a blessing in disguise, then,' Martin Southerby suggested. He smiled. 'Fairly well disguised just now.' He waved his hand at the extensive ironmongery surrounding Amy's leg. 'We had to use external fixation because the bone fragments couldn't provide adequate anchoring for pins or a plate. The soft-tissue injuries also needed major attention. Thanks to you, I got to meet the plastic surgery team last night. We had quite a party in Theatre.'

'Plastic surgery?' Amy echoed.

'There wasn't too much skin available apart from a rather badly scarred area. This fracture must have been in exactly the same place as your original injury. I'd guess that the bone was weakened at that point because it had never been satisfactorily aligned.'

'It was pretty crooked,' Amy admitted.

'You'll notice a sore patch on your other thigh. They took a split skin graft. I'm sure they'll explain it all to you later. Right now, I want to check my contribution to the repair.' The surgeon moved towards Amy's foot, suspended in the air by ropes that were attached to an overhead bed frame. He felt the pedal pulse on the top of her foot, assessed the skin temperature and checked the capillary refill by pressing the nail beds on her toes.

'Any tingling or numbness?' he queried.

'No.'

'Try wiggling your toes.'

Amy complied.

'Now push your foot against my hand.' The movement was tiny but Martin was satisfied.

'How long will I need the fixator on?' Amy asked.

'A fair while, I'm afraid. You'll be strung up in here

for anything up to four weeks and then we'll get you mobilised. You're going to need frequent dressing changes and monitoring of the soft-tissue injury, but once that's healed we'll get you going again.' He winked at Amy. 'I expect you to make a complete recovery.'

'So your reputation doesn't suffer?'

'Absolutely. Now, if you'll excuse me, I intend to finish my tour of this place that got interrupted yesterday. I suspect you'll be having a few more visitors so you shouldn't get too bored.'

The group moved away. Noel was the last to leave. 'You were lucky,' he told Amy. 'I've never seen anyone as good as Martin. He was determined to get things right no matter how long it took.' Noel shook his head in admiration. 'It was amazing.'

Jennifer appeared in the doorway. She held a huge bunch of flowers. 'I picked these out of the garden for you,' she told Amy. 'How are you feeling?'

'Not bad,' Amy assured her. 'Noel's new boss says I'll be better than ever after this. He's straightened my leg.'

'Really? Fantastic!' Jennifer beamed. 'You'll be able to go ice skating.'

'And dancing.' Amy smiled.

'But possibly not mountain biking,' Noel offered with a grin.

'You gave us an awful fright,' Jennifer told Amy. 'I was in Emergency when we heard. You should have seen Tom's face. He went as white as a sheet.'

'Really?' Amy watched Jennifer arrange the delphiniums in a tall vase.

'I swear he would have flown that helicopter himself if the paramedics hadn't invited him to go with them.'

'He hung around Theatre all night, too,' Noel told her. 'And then he sat beside your bed in Recovery until you started to wake up.'

'We all did that.' Jennifer finished arranging the flowers and returned to give Amy a hug. 'I'm so glad you're OK.'

'I might still be on crutches when you want a bridesmaid,' Amy warned.

'We'll find a best man who can carry you.' Jennifer grinned. 'In fact, we know someone who's already had some practice.'

'What, has Tom been a best man before?' Noel quipped.

Jennifer rolled her eyes. 'You know what I mean.'

Amy knew as well. She closed her eyes. She had only hazy memories of being carried from the party by Tom that night and the more recent and also fuzzy memory of being cradled in his arms yesterday when she'd been transferred to the stretcher and helicopter. She didn't want to try for a third occasion.

'Amy's tired,' she heard Jennifer tell Noel. 'We'd better go.'

'We had,' Noel agreed. 'She'll need to rest up for everyone else who wants to visit.'

Amy was astonished at the number of people who came in and out of her room during the course of that day. The staff on the orthopaedic ward were checking on her frequently. She still needed pain relief, the dressings had to be changed and the pin sites where the slim rods went through her leg to connect to the external framing had to be cleaned in what was a lengthy procedure. It was the number of people not directly involved with her care that amazed her. She'd had no idea she had so many friends. How could she have even considered leaving to work elsewhere?

Emergency department staff took it in turns to visit when they were on their breaks. Even Gareth came in and added another contribution to the rapidly expanding floral display. He smiled warmly at Amy.

'I'm delighted to note that I haven't received that letter of resignation yet.'

'I'm not going to resign,' Amy told him. 'I'm going to apply for that nurse manager's position instead.'

'Wonderful!' The head of the emergency department looked genuinely pleased.

'I might be off work for a while,' Amy said dubiously. 'Would they hold the position if I did get it?'

'I don't think there's much of an "if" there.' Gareth smiled. 'And, yes, the right person is definitely worth waiting for. It took us a while to find the perfect person to fill the permanent consultancy position, too, but everyone's happy with the choice.'

'Oh? Who got that job?' Amy enquired.

'Tom Barlow,' Gareth Harvey told her. 'Good news, isn't it?'

'He's perfect,' Amy agreed. She felt herself begin to redden. 'For the job, I mean.'

Gareth just smiled. 'Of course.'

Shane, the young man who had inadvertently caused the accident, came in to see Amy. He brought flowers, fruit and numerous heartfelt apologies. Amy assured him that he didn't need to feel so bad. She even explained to Shane about the problems her leg had caused prior to the accident.

'So I shouldn't have been up there anyway,' she admitted. 'I didn't know what I was doing and I got over-confident, trying that difficult track.'

'And the surgeon reckons it's going to be OK?'

'Better than it's been since I was ten,' Amy con-firmed. 'So I should thank you really.'

'I wouldn't go that far. It must hurt like hell.'

'It's not too bad, actually. See this button?' Amy held up the device attached to the IV line in her arm. 'If my leg gets sore I push the button and it gives me a dose of painkiller.'

Shane left when Cathy Hanson arrived. She was car-rying Jack in a front pack. 'I just heard,' she said to Amy. 'How are you feeling?'

'A bit tired,' Amy admitted.

'I won't stay long. I wanted to tell you that Jack and I are going home tomorrow.' Cathy glanced at Amy's overcrowded window and smiled. 'I told the nurses to load all my flowers on a trolley and bring them up here for you. I hope you don't get hay fever.'

'I'm not allergic to anything.' Amy grinned but her smile faded as a very unexpected visitor came through the door. Janice was carrying one of the Cellophane-wrapped baskets of fruit that the hospital gift shop spe-cialised in.

'I just popped in to say goodbye to everyone in Emergency,' Janice announced. 'And I heard about you.' She eyed the contraption around Amy's leg. 'That is truly gruesome,' she declared.

Cathy was excusing herself but Amy cast her a des-perate glance. She didn't want to be left alone with Janice. Hurriedly, she introduced the two women. Janice turned casually back to Amy.

'I haven't seen much of you lately. I thought you'd be at Noel's party but you weren't.'

'I was there,' Amy said quietly. 'I just left early.'

'Have you seen my ring?' Janice extended her left hand.

'Hard to miss.' Amy managed a smile. 'Congratulations, Janice.'

'Thanks. I know some people think it's all a bit sudden and I've just hooked the poor guy unawares, but it's not like that, you know?' Janice's smile was, for once, patently sincere. 'We just knew that we were right for each other.'

'That happened to me, too,' Cathy offered. 'When you find the right person there's not much doubt. You're very lucky, Janice.'

'I know.'

Amy closed her eyes. Maybe she should have let Cathy go. This wasn't quite the moral support she'd been hoping for. Jack woke up and started fussing. This time Amy didn't demur when Cathy excused herself. Janice went with her.

'Do you know?' Amy heard Janice say to Cathy. 'I never thought I was that interested in babies but now I can't wait. I'm going to get pregnant as soon as I can.' The voices faded as Janice giggled, but Amy could still hear her only too clearly as the women went out of the door. 'I might be already. God knows, we've been trying hard enough.'

Amy really did feel exhausted now. She asked the nursing staff to turn away any more visitors so she could sleep. It was quite dark when she awoke. The curtains in her room had been drawn and only the night light above her bed was turned on. Amy blinked, wondering where she was for a moment. The bed frame and attachments were casting eerie shadows on the ceiling.

'Are you awake, angel?'

The soft query startled Amy. She swung her head to find Tom slumped in the soft armchair beside her bed. He looked as though he'd been sitting there for a long time. 'Do you want me to call your nurse?' Tom asked, his tone one of concern. 'Do you need any pain relief?'

'No.' Amy was looking at Tom's face. Lines she had never seen before crowded his dark eyes, the colour of which was echoed in the shadows beneath them. 'What time is it?'

'Only 9 p.m. I came up as soon as I finished in Emergency. I had to bribe your nurse to let me in. I promised I'd help with your pin care and dressing change after you woke up.'

'You look awfully tired,' Amy said anxiously.

'It's been a long day,' Tom admitted. Then he smiled. 'What kept me going were all the reports I got from the people who sneaked up here to visit you. I felt a lot happier after Gareth told me how well you were doing.'

'Oh!' Amy smiled. 'Gareth told me about you getting the permanent position. Congratulations.'

'Thanks.' Tom sounded surprised. 'I thought you already knew about that. I thought everybody did. The news came through ages ago.'

'I must have missed it.' Amy's brow furrowed as Tom stifled a yawn. 'Did you get any sleep last night?'

Tom shrugged. He looked vaguely embarrassed and eyed the closed door to Amy's room. 'I should let them know you're awake, I guess.'

'Not yet,' Amy said hurriedly. 'I'm not looking forward to all that fiddling about with my leg.'

Tom glanced at the IV bag and infusion pump hanging from the pole near Amy's head. 'Give yourself a dose of morphine now,' he advised. 'I'll hang around and make sure they're not too brutal.'

'I thought you were going to help. You can't break a promise.'

'No. I couldn't do that,' Tom agreed. 'Not unless you wanted me to.'

Amy shook her head, trying to look disapproving. Did Tom remember the promise he'd made about not kissing her? He'd kept that one even if he hadn't intended to. She hadn't had the chance to let him know how willing she would have been to have that promise broken. She stared at the ceiling in the silence that fell. She heard Tom sigh lightly.

'You're tired,' she told him again. 'You should go home and get some sleep.'

Tom didn't stir. 'It's a long time since I've sat in a hospital room, worrying about someone I'm not professionally responsible for. I'd forgotten how hard it can be.'

Amy blinked. How could visiting her be comparable to watching his wife die? And Jennifer had said he'd sat up with her all night. But, then, so had Jen and Noel. The bonds of friendship were strong amongst them all.

'It must bring back some sad memories,' Amy suggested gently.

'Nothing I can't deal with,' Tom said slowly. 'I realised they had finally gone that day when Jason Kingsley died.' He smiled ruefully at Amy. 'I lived with much more powerful ghosts for a long time, Amy. Even the move to Chicago didn't obliterate them completely. I thought I would escape them by coming back to New Zealand. I hadn't expected to resurrect even older ones by meeting Nigel again. Last I'd heard, he was intending to settle overseas. I thought he would be long gone from Christchurch.'

'But he wasn't.'

'I was a bit shocked to learn he was working in the Queen Mary when I arrived. I went to his house that night to let him know I was in town and that I had every intention of keeping our relationship quiet. I hoped he would want to do the same. I hadn't expected things to be quite so difficult.' Tom chuckled. 'That was your doing, Amy Brooks. If I hadn't found you loitering in that garden I would have just slipped away. I had no desire at all to gatecrash Nigel's engagement party.'

'I wouldn't have married him, you know,' Amy stated. 'I knew all along it wasn't the right thing to do. I just didn't want to admit it.'

'You might have taken longer to admit it without a bit of encouragement,' Tom said. 'You might have left it too late and that was a risk I couldn't afford to take.'

Amy felt suddenly shy. 'Why not?'

Tom sat forward in the chair. He took hold of Amy's hand and his dark eyes were locked on her face. 'Don't you know the answer to that, Amy?'

Amy shook her head very slowly, without breaking the contact with those eyes. She wanted to wrap herself in that gaze and never escape.

'I love you,' Tom said simply. He smiled crookedly. 'I fell in love with you when I saw you talking to that statue. Or maybe it was when I heard that drunk Irishman proposing to you in Emergency. Your blush was rather enchanting.'

Amy shook herself mentally to try and clear her sudden confusion. The joy Tom's declaration had given her had to be shelved for the moment. She tried to concentrate on what she knew had to be said.

'It must have made things a bit difficult for you,' she began.

'It was a bit tricky,' Tom agreed. He was still smiling. 'I hadn't bargained on you finding out about me sabotaging that date with Nigel, but it was a desperate move on my part and I figured that all was fair in love and war. I wasn't expecting you to hear about my marriage like that either.' He squeezed Amy's hand. 'I would have told you myself, of course. There were just more important issues to get sorted first.'

'Like what?'

'Like your conviction that it would be so easy to put me off. I started to wonder if it was just an excuse to get rid of me.'

'What was?' It was more difficult to concentrate than Amy had anticipated. She was losing the plot somewhere along the line.

'Your tin leg,' Tom said casually. 'You didn't really think it would have been enough to change my mind about you, did you?'

'It's happened before.' Amy pulled her gaze away from Tom. 'My first boyfriend pretended it didn't bother him but he ran a mile as soon as he got the opportunity. I was very careful not to let anybody see my leg after that.'

'I can see it now,' Tom said, a little smugly.

'Everybody can see it now.' Amy laughed. 'And they've all been in here today to have a good look.'

'You must be exhausted,' Tom said reluctantly. 'I should go.'

'I'm fine,' Amy said quickly. 'But don't feel you have to stay, Tom. Only if you want to.'

'Of course I want to stay,' Tom said impatiently. 'Haven't you been listening, Amy Brooks? I want to stay beside you for every possible minute for the rest of my life.'

'Oh.' It took a few seconds for the statement to register properly. 'Does Janice know that?'

'Why the hell should she?' Tom sounded bewildered.

'Some people might consider it polite.'

'What *are* you talking about, Amy?'

'Well,' Amy said carefully, 'if I was engaged to somebody who really wanted to spend his life with somebody else, I think I would rather know about it before there were any major complications.'

Tom looked interested now. 'What sort of complications?'

'Marriage, for one,' Amy said confidently. 'And babies, of course.'

Tom was silent for a short time. 'How much morphine have you had tonight, Amy?'

'Not much. I've been asleep.'

'You can't have had any access to champagne in here,' Tom mused. 'But you seem to be out of your mind all the same, Amy Brooks. Just who do you think Janice is engaged *to*?'

Amy's jaw dropped a little. 'You, of course.'

Tom shook his head. 'Why would *I* be engaged to Janice Healey?'

Amy smiled understandingly. 'Maybe you love her, too.'

'I don't even particularly like the woman,' Tom declared.

'She looks like Lucy,' Amy said defensively. 'You said so yourself.'

'Yes, but she doesn't look anything like you, angel.' Tom's face loomed close as he leaned over Amy and stared at her intently. 'It's *you* I'm in love with. *Only. You.*' He enunciated the last two words with deliberate care. 'I'm not bothered about being engaged to you. We could just skip that part and get married instead if you like.'

'Who's Janice engaged to, then?' Amy wasn't going to be distracted by the proximity of Tom's lips.

'Some forty-five-year-old lawyer. She met him when he came in to have his appendix out. Stephen some-body.'

'Parks,' Amy whispered. Remembering her assumption that Janice would consider Stephen too old for her, Amy felt ashamed. They were obviously genuinely in love. Then she said in confusion, 'But what about the party?'

'The party?' Tom also seemed to be concentrating. He sat down on the side of the bed. 'She gets around, doesn't she?' Tom sounded impressed. 'I didn't even see Janice at Nigel's house.'

'Not Nigel's party. Noel's.' Amy sighed. This was hard work. 'I saw you arrive. Janice was flashing her ring at everybody and hanging onto your arm.'

'Janice was hanging on to everybody's arms. She wanted to make sure they didn't escape before they admired the ring. I happened to arrive at the same time. Her fiancé turned up about the time you disappeared.'

'But everybody was congratulating you.'

'About the job.' Tom was grinning now. 'That was the day the news of the permanent consultancy position came through. Plus, I'd bought the house.' He peered at Amy. 'I hope you remember the house as well as you seem to remember everything else.'

'Oh, yes.' Amy nodded. 'It's a lovely house.' She was drifting happily now—and it had little to do with the morphine. 'It's a bit isolated, though. You'll have a lot of travelling to do for all your squash games and tennis matches and so on.'

'I'm retiring,' Tom told her. 'As of now. I'm planning to stay home and become very unfit.' He was leaning closer again.

'You wouldn't do that.'

'Maybe not completely,' Tom admitted. 'But I'll certainly cut down. I got into the habit of too much physical activity and being in a crowd of people as a survival mechanism after Lucy died. I didn't want too much time alone. I thought I would never want to be alone again. Until I stood in that house with you.'

'You weren't alone,' Amy pointed out.

'Exactly. And I never want to be alone again.'

Amy had lost the plot again. 'You're not making any sense,' she told Tom firmly. 'And it's me that's supposed to be out of my head.'

'Maybe this will make sense.' Tom cupped Amy's chin and kissed her gently. Then he kissed her again and Amy was transported back in time to that forest cottage. Only this time the desire to be touched was even stronger. Strong enough to make her cry out against Tom's mouth. He drew back instantly.

'I've hurt you,' he exclaimed. 'God, I'm sorry, Amy.'

'I'm not hurt,' Amy assured him. 'I'm...uh...' Amy could feel herself blushing.

'Frustrated?' Tom grinned wolfishly.

'You could say that.' Amy smiled up at him. 'I love you, Tom Barlow. I want to be with you for the rest of my life.' She bit her lip. 'And right now I would quite like your body as well.' She groaned softly. 'I'm going to be tied up in this awful contraption for weeks.'

Tom's smile was wicked. 'I would quite like your body as well, angel, but we'll just have to be patient. We're going to have plenty of time to talk and get to know each other extremely well.' His breath teased her lips as he leaned forward again. 'We're also going to get extremely good at kissing.' His lips were so close now Amy could feel their movement against her own.

'Heaven, I'm afraid,' Tom whispered, 'will just have to wait.'

MILLS & BOON®

Makes any time special™

Mills & Boon publish 29 new titles every month. Select from...

Modern Romance™   Tender Romance™

Sensual Romance™

Medical Romance™ Historical Romance™

MAT2

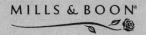

FREE!

4 Books
and a surprise gift!

We would like to take this opportunity to thank you for reading this Mills & Boon® book by offering you the chance to take FOUR more specially selected titles from the Medical Romance™ series absolutely FREE! We're also making this offer to introduce you to the benefits of the Reader Service™ —

- ★ FREE home delivery
- ★ FREE gifts and competitions
- ★ FREE monthly Newsletter
- ★ Books available before they're in the shops
- ★ Exclusive Reader Service discounts

Accepting these FREE books and gift places you under no obligation to buy; you may cancel at any time, even after receiving your free shipment. Simply complete your details below and return the entire page to the address below. *You don't even need a stamp!*

YES! Please send me 4 free Medical Romance books and a surprise gift. I understand that unless you hear from me, I will receive 6 superb new titles every month for just £2.49 each, postage and packing free. I am under no obligation to purchase any books and may cancel my subscription at any time. The free books and gift will be mine to keep in any case.

M1ZEB

Ms/Mrs/Miss/Mr ....Initials....................................
BLOCK CAPITALS PLEASE

Surname...

Address...

....

....Postcode ....

Send this whole page to:
UK: The Reader Service, FREEPOST CN8I, Croydon, CR9 3WZ
EIRE: The Reader Service, PO Box 4546, Kilcock, County Kildare (stamp required)